Solomon Spaulding

**The Manuscript Story**

Solomon Spaulding

**The Manuscript Story**

ISBN/EAN: 9783337318086

Printed in Europe, USA, Canada, Australia, Japan

Cover: Foto ©Raphael Reischuk / pixelio.de

More available books at **www.hansebooks.com**

*The*

# "*Manuscript Story,*"

*of*

### *Reverend Solomon Spalding;*

*or*

### "*Manuscript Found.*"

*From a verbatim copy of the original now in the Library of Oberlin College, Ohio; including correspondence touching the Manuscript, its preservation and transmission until it came into the hands of the publishers.*

*LAMONI, IOWA:*
*Printed and published by the Reorganized Church of Jesus Christ of Latter Day Saints.*

# THE "MANUSCRIPT STORY."

### A Verbatim Copy from the Original.

HEREWITH we present to the reader the notorious "Manuscript Story" ["Manuscript Found"], of the Reverend Solomon Spalding. What gives this document prominence is the fact that for the past fifty years it has been made to do duty by the opposers of the Book of Mormon as the source, the root, and the inspiration, by and from which Joseph Smith and Sydney Rigdon wrote the Book of Mormon. It has been popularly and persistently claimed that the plan, subject matter, including prominent names and localites, history of the origin of the aboriginal races of America, with their arts and sciences, civilizations and customs, were identical in this "Manuscript Found" and in the Book of Mormon. Thousands have believed this false and foolish statement, without giving its truth or falsity an hour's fair and unprejudiced investigation, and then fought the book and the church with a readiness and a zeal almost without a parallel. And now that this veritable "Manuscript Found," with an unbroken chain of evidence proving its identity and running back to E. D. Howe, D. P. Hurlbut, Spalding's "old trunk," and so back to Pittsburg, Conneaut, and to the very pen of Solomon Spalding, has by the providence of God been furnished us, and that, too, by those not of the church, we take pleasure in exhibiting in the sunlight of solid facts, this hob-goblin of the pulpit, this "nigger-in-the-woodpile" of the press and the forum, that with which they have fooled and frightened the masses and blinded those inquiring into the origin and character of the Book of Mormon.

This seeming huge hindrance and insurmountable obstacle which is always thrown in the way of the investigator with all the skill and power that craft and cunning and malice and fear and blind zeal can invent and command, vanishes from the presence of this original witness in the case; for when it speaks it reveals the flimsiness and falsity of the claim that it was in any way or in any sense the origin of the Book of Mormon, or that there is the least likeness between the two. This newly found "missing link" completes the chain of evidence which proves that the "Manuscript Found" never was and never could be made the occasion, cause, or germ of the Book of Mormon.

Mr. Spalding has been exalted by the opposers of the Latter Day Saints to the very pinnacle of fame, as a very learned, very moral, and very pious man. It is fortunate that his true measure and worth in respect to his learning, his morals, and his piety, is now furnished us in this "Manuscript Story." God judges men by their works, and it is wise for men to judge of each other after this manner. And when we estimate Mr. Spalding by the character of his work as exhibited in this document, we must grade him down to a very low level, whether in respect to scholarship, mental power, moral purity, or pious attainments and tendencies.

The following correspondence explains the manner in which the manuscript was preserved and placed in the hands of the present publishers.

———

The following from the *Bibliotheca Sacra* was republished in many leading journals east and west, among them the *Herald* of Grinnell, Iowa; the *Western Watchman*, Eureka, California; the *New York Observer*, and Frank Leslie's *Sunday Magazine*.

"The theory of the origin of the Book of Mormon in the traditional manuscript of Solomon Spaulding, will probably have to be relinquished. That manuscript is doubtless now in the possession of Mr. L. L. Rice, of Honolulu, Hawaiian Islands, formerly an anti-slavery editor in Ohio, and for many years State Printer, at Columbus. During a recent visit to Honolulu, I suggested to Mr. Rice that he might have valuable anti-slavery documents in his possession, which he would be willing to contribute to the rich collection already in the Oberlin College Library. In pursuance of this suggestion, Mr. Rice began looking over his old pamphlets and papers, and at length came upon an old, worn, and faded manuscript of about one hundred and seventy-five pages, small quarto, purporting to be a history of the migrations and conflicts of the ancient Indian Tribes, which occupied the territory now belonging to the States of New York, Ohio, and Kentucky. On the last page of this manuscript is a certificate and signature, giving the names of several persons known to the signer, who have assured him that to their personal knowledge the manuscript was the writing of Solomon Spaulding. Mr. Rice has no recollection how or when this manuscript came into his possession. It was enveloped in a coarse piece of wrapping paper, and endorsed in Mr. Rice's handwriting, 'A Manuscript Story.'

"There seems no reason to doubt that this is the long-lost story. Mr. Rice, myself, and others, compared it with the Book of Mormon, and could detect no resemblance between the two, in general or in detail. There seems to be no name or incident common to the two. The solemn style of the Book of Mormon, in imitation of the English Scriptures, does not appear in the manuscript. The only resemblance is in the fact that both profess to set forth the history of lost tribes. Some other explanation of the origin of the Book of Mormon must be found, if any explanation is required." Signed, James H. Fairchild.

The letter below was written in answer to our suggestion that the Manuscript be sent for safe keeping to some Historical Society in Chicago, Illinois.

HONOLULU, Sandwich Islands, March 28, 1885.

MR. JOSEPH SMITH:

The Spaulding Manuscript in my possession came into my hands in this wise. In 1839–40 my partner and myself bought of E. D. Howe the *Painesville Telegraph*, published at Painesville, Ohio. The transfer of the printing department, types, press, &c., was accompanied with a large collection, of books, manuscripts, &c., this manuscript of Spaulding among the rest. So, you see, it has been in my possession over forty years. But I never examined it, or knew the character of it, until some six or eight months since. The wrapper was marked, "Manuscript Story—Conneaut Creek." The wonder is, that in some of my movements, I did not destroy or burn it with a large amount of rubbish that had accumulated from time to time.

It happened that President Fairchild was here on a visit, at the time I discovered the contents of it, and it was examined by him and others with much curiosity. Since President Fairchild published the fact of its existence in my possession, I have had applications for it from half a dozen sources, each applicant seeming to think that he or she was entitled to it. Mr. Howe says when he was getting up a book to expose Mormonism as a fraud at an early day, when the Mormons had their headquarters at Kirtland, he obtained it from some source, and it was inadvertently transferred with the other effects of his printing office. A. B. Deming, of Painesville, who is also getting up some kind of a book I believe on Mormonism, wants me to send it to him. Mrs. Dickinson, of Boston, claiming to be a relative of Spaulding, and who is getting up a book to show that he was the real author of the Book of Mormon, wants it. She thinks, at least, it should be sent to Spaulding's daughter, a Mrs. Somebody—but she does not inform me where she lives. Deming says that Howe borrowed it when he was getting up his book, and did not return it, as he should have done, etc.

This Manuscript does not purport to be "a story of the Indians formerly occupying this continent;" but is a history of the wars between the Indians of Ohio and Kentucky, and their progress in civilization, etc. It is certain that this Manuscript is not the origin of the Mormon Bible, whatever some other manuscript may have been. The only similarity between them, is, in the manner in which each purports to have been found—one in a cave on Conneaut Creek—the other in a hill in Ontario County, New York. There is no identity of names, of persons, or places; and there is no similarity of style between them. As I told Mr. Deming, I should as soon think the Book of Revelations was written by the author of Don Quixote, as that the writer of this Manuscript was the author of the Book of Mormon. Deming says Spaulding made three copies of "Manuscript Found," one of which Sidney Rigdon stole from a printing-office in Pittsburg. You can probably tell better than I can, what ground there is for such an allegation.

As to this Manuscript, I can not see that it can be of any use to any body, except the Mormons, to show that IT is not the original of the Mormon Bible. But that would not settle the claim that some other manuscript of Spaulding was the original of it. I propose to hold it in my own hands for a while, to see if it can not be put to some good use. Deming and Howe inform me that its existence is exciting great interest in that region. I am under a tacit, but not a positive pledge to President Fairchild, to deposit it eventually in the Library of Oberlin College. I shall be free from that pledge, when I see an opportunity to put it to a better use. Yours, etc.,

L. L. RICE.

P. S.—Upon reflection, since writing the foregoing, I am of the opinion that no one who reads this Manuscript will give credit to the story that Solomon Spaulding was in any wise the author of the Book of Mormon.  It is unlikely that any one who wrote so elaborate a work as the Mormon Bible, would spend his time in getting up so shallow a story as this, which at best is but a feeble imitation of the other.  Finally I am more than half convinced that this is his only writing of the sort, and that any pretence that Spaulding was in any sense the author of the other, is a sheer fabrication.  It was easy for anybody who may have seen this, or heard anything of its contents, to get up the story that they were identical.          L. L. R.

---

HONOLULU, Sandwich Islands,
May 14, 1885.

MR. JOSEPH SMITH;

*Dear Sir:* I am greatly obliged to you for the information concerning Mormonism, in your letters of April 30 and May 2.  As I am in no sense a Mormonite, of course it is a matter of curiosity, mainly, that I am interested in the history of Mormonism.

Two things are true concerning this manuscript in my possession:  First, it is a genuine writing of Solomon Spaulding; and second, it is *not* the original of the Book of Mormon.

My opinion is, from all I have seen and learned, that this is the *only* writing of Spaulding, and there is no foundation for the statement of Deming and others, that Spaulding made another story, more elaborate, of which several copies were written, one of which Rigdon stole from a printing-office in Pittsburg, etc.  Of course I can not be as certain of this, as of the other two points.  One theory is, that Rigdon, or some one else, saw this manuscript, or heard it read, and from the hints it conveyed, got up the other and more elaborate writing on which the Book of Mormon was founded.  Take that for what it is worth.  It don't seem to me very likely.

You may be at rest as to my putting the manuscript into the possession of any one who will mutilate it, or use it for a bad purpose.  I shall have it deposited in the Library of Oberlin College, in Ohio, to be at the disposal for reading of any one who may wish to peruse it; but not to be removed from that depository.  My friend, President Fairchild, may be relied on as security for the safe-keeping of it.  It will be sent there in July, by a friend who is going there to "take to himself a wife." Meantime, I have made a literal copy of the entire document— errors of orthography, grammar, erasures, and all—which I shall keep in my possession, so that any attempt to mutilate it will be of easy detection and exposure. Oberlin is a central place, in the vicinity of Conneaut, where the manuscript was written.

I have had an idea, sometimes, that it is due to the Mormons to have a copy of it, if they took interest in it enough to publish it. As it is only of interest as showing that it is not the original of the Book of Mormon, no one else is likely to wish it for publication.

Miss Dickinson, whom you call a granddaughter of Solomon Spaulding, represents herself to me as his grandniece: "My great uncle, Rev. Solomon Spaulding," she writes.

Rev. Dr. Hyde, President of the Institution, in this place, for training Native Missionaries for Micranesia, (a very prominent and successful institution), has written an elaborate account of this manuscript, and of Mormonism, and sent it for publication in the *Congregationalist*, of Boston. I presume it will be published, and you will be interested in reading it.

Very respectfully, yours,<br>L. L. RICE.

---

In a postscript Mr. Rice says he found the following endorsement on the Manuscript:

"The writings of Solomon Spaulding proved by Aron Wright, Oliver Smith, John N. Miller and others. The testimonies of the above gentlemen are now in my possession.

(Signed)      D. P. HURLBUT."

---

COPY OF MR. RICE'S LETTER.

HONOLULU, H. I., June 12, 1885.

PRESIDENT J. H. FAIRCHILD:

Herewith I send to you the Solomon Spalding Manuscript, to be deposited in the Library of Oberlin College, for reference by any one who may be desirous of seeing or examining it. As a great deal of inquiry has been made about it since it became known that it was in my possession, I deem it proper that it be deposited for safe keeping, where any one interested in it, whether Mormon or Anti-Mormon, may examine it. It has been in my possession forty-six years—from 1839 to 1885—and for forty-four years of that time no one examined it, and I was not aware of the character of its contents. I send it to you enclosed in the same paper wrapper, and tied with the same string that must have enclosed it for near half a century—certainly during the forty-six years since it came into my possession. I have made and retain in my possession a correct literal copy of it, errors of orthography, of grammar, erasures and all. I may allow the Mormons of Utah to print it from this copy, which they are anxious to do; and a delegation is now in the Islands, awaiting my decision on this point. They claim that they are entitled to whatever benefit they may derive from its publication; and it seems to me there is some justice in that claim. Whether it will relieve them in any measure, from the imputation that Solomon Spalding was the author of the Book of Mormon, I do not attempt to decide. It devolves upon their opponents to show that there are or were other writings of Spalding—since it is evident that this writing is not the original of the Mormon Bible.

Truly, yours, etc.,

L. L. RICE.

P. S.—The words "Solomon Spaulding's Writings" in ink on the wrapper were written by me, after I became aware of the contents. The words "Manuscript Story—Conneaut Creek," in faint penciling, were as now when it came into my possession.

---

OBERLIN COLLEGE, Oberlin, Ohio,<br>July 23, 1885.

I have this day delivered to Mr. E. L. Kelley a copy of the Manuscript of Solomon Spaulding, sent from Honolulu by Mr. L. L. Rice, to the Library of Oberlin College, for safe-keeping, and now in my care. The copy was prepared at Mr. Kelley's request, under my supervision, and is, as I believe, an exact

:ranscript of the original manuscript, including erasures, mis-
spellings, etc.                JAS. H. FAIRCHILD,
                     Prest. of Oberlin College.

KIRTLAND, Ohio, July 24, 1885.
PRES. W. W. BLAIR, Lamoni, Iowa:
Herewith I transmit to you the copy of the Spaulding Manuscript prepared by President Fairchild as attested by him,
together with his certificate, and photograph sheets.
                       E. L. KELLEY.

Words and sentences underlined were stricken out in the Manuscript.
Places marked thus - - - - the copy was illegible.

## INTRODUCTION.

NEAR the west Bank of the Coneaught River there
are the remains of an ancient fort. As I was walking and forming various conjectures respecting the
character situation & numbers of those people who
far exceeded the present Indians in works of art and
inginuety, I hapned to tread on a flat stone. This
was at a small distance from the fort, & it lay on the
top of a great small mound of Earth exactly horizontal. The face of it had a singular appearance. I
discovered a number of characters, which appeared
to me to be letters, but so much effaced by the ravages of time, that I could not read the inscription.
With the assistance of a leaver I raised the stone.
But you may easily conjecture my astonishment
when I discovered that its ends and sides rested on
stones & that it was designed as a cover to an arti-

ficial Cave. I found by examining that its sides were lined with stones built in a connical form with - - - - - down, & that it was about eight feet deep. Determined to investigate the design of this extraordinary work of antiquity, I prepared myself with the necessary requisites for that purpose and descended to the Bottom of the Cave. Observing one side to be perpendicular nearly three feet from the bottom, I began to inspect that part with accuracy. Here I noticed a big flat stone fixed in the form of a doar. I immediately tore it down and Lo, a cavity within the wall presented itself it being about three feet in diamiter from side to side and about two feet high. Within this cavity I found an earthern Box with a cover which shut it perfectly tite. The Box was two feet in length one & half in breadth & one & three inches in diameter. My mind filled with awful sensations which crowded fast upon me would hardly permit my hands to remove this venerable deposit, but curiosity soon gained the assendency & the box was taken & raised to open it. When I had removed the Cover I found that it contained twenty-eight rolls of parchment-&-that when - - - appeared to be manuscrips written in eligant hand with Roman Letters & in the Latin Language.

They were written on a variety of Subjects. But the Roll which principally attracted my attention contained a history of the author's life & that part of America which extends along the great Lakes & the waters of the Mississippy.

Extracts of the most interesting and important matters contined in this Roll I take the liberty to publish.

Gentle Reader, tread lightly on the ashes of the venerable dead. Thou must know that this Country was once inhabited by great and powerful nations considerably civilized & skilled in the arts of war, & that on ground where thou now treadest many a bloody Battle hath been fought, & heroes by thousands have been made to bite the dust.

In the history given of these nations by my author you will find nothing but what will correspond with the natural sentiments we should form on viewing the innumerable remains of antiquity which are scattered over an extensive Country. This is an evidence of the author's impartiality and veracity. But if any should pretend that the whole story is fictitious or fabulous

To publish a translation of every particular circumstance mentioned by our author would produce a volume too expensive for the general class of readers, But should this attempt to throw off the veil which has seculded our view from the transactions o. nations who for ages have been extinct, meet the approbation of the public, I shall then be happy to gratify the more inquisitive and learned part of my readers by a more minute publication. Apprehensive that skeptical illiberal or superstitous minds may censure this performance with great accrimony I have only to remark that they will be deprived of a great fund of entertainment - - - of a contrary disposition will obtain. My compassion will be excited more than my resentment and there the contest will end.

Now, Gentle Reader, the Translator who wishes well to thy present and thy future existence entreats thee to peruse this volume with a clear head a pure heart and a candid mind. If thou shalt then find that thy head and thy heart are both improved it will afford him more satisfaction than the approbation of ten thousand who have received no benefit.

And now permit me to admonish thee that if thou shouldst reside in or travil thro' any part of the Country

## CHAPT. I.

### AN EPITOME OF THE AUTHOR'S LIFE & OF HIS ARIVAL IN AMERICA.

AS IT is possible that in some future age this part of the Earth will be inhabited by Europians & a history of its present inhabitants would be a valuable acquisition I proceed to write one & deposit it in a box secured - - - so that the ravages of time will have no effect upon it that you may know the author I will give a succint account of his life and of the cause of his arival which I have extracted from a manuscript which will be deposited with this history.

My name was is Fabius The family name I sustain is Fabius, being decended from the illustrious general of that name. I was born at Rome & received my education under the tuition of a very Learned Master. At the time that Constantine arived at that city and had overcome his enimies & and was firmly seated on the throne of the Roman empire I was introduced to him as a young Gentleman of genius and learning & as being worthy of the favourable notice of his imperial majesty. He gave me the appointment of one of his secritaries, & such were the gracious intimations which he frequently gave me of his high approbation of my conduct that I was happy in my station.

One day he says to me Fabius you must go to Brittian & carry an important - - - to the general of our army there - - - sail in a vessel & return when she returns. Preparation was made instantly and we sailed - - - The vessel laden with provisions for the army - - - Cloath-knives and other impliments for their use had now arived near the coast of Britain when a tremendous storm arose & drove us into the midst of the boundless Ocean. Soon the whole crew became lost & bewildered. They knew not the direction for to the rising Sun or polar Star, for the heavens were covered with clouds; & darkness had spread 'her sable mantle over the face of the raging deep. Their minds were filled with consternation and despair. & unanimously agreed that What could we do? How be extrecated from the insatiable jaws of a watry tomb.. Then it was that we felt our absolute dependence on that Almighty & gracious Being who holds the winds & floods in - - hands. From him alone could we expect deliverance. To him our most fervent desires assended. Prostrate & on bended nees we poured forth incessant Supplication & even Old Ocean appeared to sympathize in our distress by returning the echo of our vociforos Cries & lamenta-

tions.  After being driven five days with incridable
velocity before the furious wind the storm abated in
its violance.  but still the strong wind blew strong
in the strong as I now believe in the same direction.
Doubtful whether the wind had not changed her point
we give the ship full sail & let her drive.  On the
sixth day after, the storm wholly subsided, the sun
rose clear and the heavens once more appeared ·
to smile.  Inexpressible was the consternation of all
the crew.  they found themselves in the midst of a
vast Ocean. ˙ No prospect of returning.  All was
lost.  The wind blowing westwardly, & the presump-
tion was that it had been blowing in that direction during the whole of the storm.  No pen can
paint the dolorious cries & lamentations of the
poor mariners, for the loss of friends for the loss
of everything they held most - - - At length a
Mariner stept - - - the midst and proclaimed.
Attend O friends & listen to my words.  A voice from
on high hath penetrated my soul & the inspiration of
the Almighty hath bid me proclaim.  Let your sails
be wide spread & the gentle winds will soon waft you
into a safe harbor.  a Country where you will find
hospitality.  Quick as the lightnings flash joy
sparkled in every countenance.  A Hymn of Thanks-
giving spontaniously burst forth from their lips.  In
full confidence that the divine prediction would be
accomplished they extoled the loving kindness and
tender mercies of their God & promised by the assistance of his grace to make ample return of Gratitude.
On the fifth day after this we came in sight of sand,
we entered a spacious river & continued sailing up

the - - - many leagues until we came in view of a
town. Every heart now palpitated with joy, & loud
shouts of gladness expressed the enthusiastic trans-
ports of our souls. We anchored within a small distance from shore. Immediately the natives ran with
apparent signs of surprize & astonishment to the bank
of the River. After viewing us for some time, &
receiving signs of Friendship, they appeared to hold
a counsel for a few minutes. Their King then stept
forward to the edge of the bank, & proffered us the
hand of friendship, & by significant gestures invited
us to Land, promising us protection and hospitality
We now found ourselves once more on terra firma, &
were conducted by the king & four chiefs into the
town whilst the multitude followed after, shouting
& performing many odd jesticulations. The King
ordered an entertainment to be prepared for his new
friends which consisted of - - - fish boiled beans
& samp - - - The whole was placed under a wide-
,spreading Oak in wooden dishes A large clam shell &
a Stone Knife were provided for each one. The king
then came forward with about twenty of his principal
subjects, & con seated us (being about twenty in
number) & seated us by the side of our repast. He
& his company then took seats in front. After
waving his hand & bowing all fell to eating & a more
delicious repast we never enjoyed. The repast being
finished, our attention was called to a collection of
about one thousand men & women who had formed a
ring & invited our company to come forward into the
midst. After gazing upon us sometime with surprize
we were permitted to withdraw & to take our stand in

the Ring. About forty in number then walked into
the midle of the Ring & began a song with but a dis-
cordant and hedious modification of sounds, & such
frantic jesticulations of body that it seemed that
chaos had bro't her furies to set the world in an
uproar. And an uproar it was in a short time for the
whole company fell to dancing, shouting, whooping,
& screaming at intervals, then dancing jumping &
tumbling with many indescribable distortions in their
countanance & indelicate jestures. In fact, they
appeared more lik a company of devils than human
Beings. This lasted about one hour. They then
took their places in a circle & at a signal given gave
three most tremendous whoops, they then instantly
dispersed playing many antike capers & making such
a confused medly of sound by skreaming, whooping,
screaching like owls, Barking like dogs & wolves &
bellowing croaking like Bullfrogs, that my brain
seemed to be turned topseturvy, & for some time I
could scarce believe that they belonged to the human
species.

## CHAPT. II

### AN ACCOUNT OF THE SETTLEMENT OF THE SHIP'S
### COMPANY & MANY PARTICULARS RESPECT-
### ING THE NATIVES.

As no alternative now remained but either to make
the desperate attempt to return across the wide boistrous Ocean, or to take up our residence in a country
in a land of savages inhabited by savages & wild

ferocious beasts, we did not long hesitate. We held a solemn treaty with the King & all the chiefs of his nation. They agreed to cede to us a tract of excellent land on the north part of the town on which was six wigwams & engaged perpetual amity & hospitality & the protection of our lives & property. In consideration of this grant we cave them fifty yards of scarlet cloth & fifty knives With this present they were highly pleased.

Arrangements must now be made for - - - settlement. Vessel & cargo had received no material damage & by striping the vessel of its plank we could erect a house in which we could deposite the whole cargo in safety. All hands were immediately employed, some in procuring timber which we hued on two sides & then locked together, some in procuring shingles & some in striping the vessel of its plank; & having a large quantity of nails on board, in ten days we finished a very convenient store-house, sufficiently spacious to receive the whole cargo. We also built a small house adjoining which was to be the habitation of the Captain & myself. Having secured all our property, we then found it necessary to establish some regulations for the government of our little society. The Captain whose name was Lucian & myself were appointed judges in all matters of controversy & managers of the public property to make bargains with the natives & barter such articles as we did not need for necessaries. As we all professed The next thing to be done was to to believe in the religion of Jesus Christ we unanimously chose Tro-

janus, the mate of the ship, a pious good man to be
our minister, to lead our devotions every morning &
evening & on the Lords day

But now a most singular & delicate subject presented itself for consideration. Seven young women
we had on board as passenjers to viset certain friends
in Brittian. Three of them were ladies of rank & the
rest were healthy bucksom lassies. Whilst deliber-
ating on this subject a mariner arose whom we called
Droll Tom Hark ye, shipmates says he. Whilst
tossed on the foming billows what brave son of
Neptune had any more regard for a woman than a
Sturgeon, but now we are all safely anchored on
Terra firma, our sails furled & ship keeled up, I
have a huge longing for some of those rosy dames.
But willing to take my chance with my shipmates, I
propose that they should make their choice of hus-
bands. The plan was instantly adopted. As the
choice fell on the young women they had a consultation on the subject, & in a short time made
known the result. Droll Tom was rewarded for
his benevolent proposal with one of the most
sprightly, rosy dames in the company. Three other
of the most cheerful, resolute mariners were chosen
by the other three bucksom Lassies. The three
young Ladies of rank fixed their choice on the
Captain the Mate & myself. Happy indeed in my
partner, I had formed an high esteem of the excellent qualities of her mind The young Lady who
chose me for a partner was possessed of every
attractive charm both of body & mind. We united

heart & hand with the fairest prospect of enjoying every delight & gratification which are attendant on the connubial state.  Thus ended the affair.
You may well conceive our singular situation.  The
six poor fellows who were doomed to live in a state
of celibacy or accept of savage dames, discovered
a little chagrin & anxiety.  However, they consoled
themselves with the idea of living in families, where
they would enjoy the company of the fair sex, &
be relieved from the work which belongs to the
department of women.

Our community might be said to be one family,
tho' we lived in separate houses situate near each
other  The property was common stock.  what
was produced by our labor was likewise to be common.  All subject to the distribution of the judges,
who were to attend to each family & to see that
propper industry & econimy were practised by all.

The Captain & myself, attended with our fair part-
ners & two mariners, repaired to the new habitation,
which consisted of. two convenient apartments.
After having partook of an elligant dinner & drank a
bottle of excellent wine our Spirits were exhilerated
& the deep gloom which beclouded our minds evaporated.  The Captain assuming his wonted cheerfulness, made the following address.  "My sweet, good
"soul'd fellows, we have now commenced a new voy-
"age.  Not such as bro't us over mountain billows to
"this butt end of the world.  No, no, our voige is on
"dry land, & now we must take care that we have
"sufficient ballast for the riging.  Every hand on
"board this ship must clasp hands & condesend to each

"others humour.    This will promote good cheer &
"smooth the raging billows of life.    Surrounded by
"innumerable hordes of human beings, who resemble
"in manners the Orang outang, let us keep aloof
"from them & not embark in the same matrimonial
"ship with them.    At the same time, we will treat
"them with good cheer & inlighten their dark souls
"with good instruction.    By continuing a different
"people & prefering our customs, manners, religion
"& arts & sciences & other things another Italy will
"grow up in this wilderness, & we shall be celebrated
"as the fathers of a great & happy nation."

May God bless your soul, says one of the mariners,
what would you have us do who have had the woful
luck not to get mates, to cheer our poor souls &
warm our bodies.    Methinks I could pick out a
healthy plum Lass from the copper colored tribe that
by washing & scrubing her fore & aft & upon the
labbord & stabbord sides she would become a wholesome bedfellow.    I think, may it please your honour,
that I could gradually pump my notions into her
head & make her a good shipmate for the cupboard &
as good hearted a Christian as any of your white
damsels & upon my Soul I warrant you if we have
children, by feeding them with good fare, & keeping
them clean, they will be as plump & as fair & nearly
as white as your your honours children.    Upon this I
filled the bottle with wine & observing to honest Crito
that he was at liberty to make the experiment if he
could find a fair - - - to his liking.    I then
expressed the the sweet pleasure I received from the

addresses of the speakers & wished drank success to the new voige. All drank plentifully, & the exhileration produced the greatest cheerfulness & hilarity. By this time the Sun had hid his head below the horizon & darkness invited all the animal creation to sleep & rest. We retired two & two, hand in hand. Ladies heads a little awri, blushing like the morn & - - - - But I forgot to mention that our society passed a resolution to build a church in the in the midst of our vilage.

## CHAPT. III.

### MANY PARTICULARS RESPECTING THE NATIVES.

INTEREST as well as curiosity invited an acquaintance with our new neighbours. They were called in their Language Deliwanucks. They were Tall, bodies weel proportioned, strait limbs, complections of a brownish hue broad cheek bones, black wild roling eyes, & hair black & course. To strangers they were both - - - true to their engagements, ardent in their friendship, but to enimies implacable, cruel & barbarous in the extreme. Innumerable hordes of this description of people were scattered over an extensive country, who gained their living by hunting the elk, the deer & a great variety of other wild animals by fishing & fowling & by raising corn, beans & squashes Shooting the arrow, flinging stones, wrestling, jumping, hoping, and runing were their principal amusements, & prizes would often be staked as a reward to the conqueror. Their cloathing consisted of skins dressed with the hair on, but in warm

weather only the middle part of their bodies were
incumbered with any covering. The one half of the
head of the men was shaved & painted with red & the
one half of the face was painted with black. The
head was adorned with feathers of various kinds, &
their ears & noses were adorned ornamented with
rings formed formed from the sinues of certain animals, on which were suspended smooth stones of
different coulors. Thus cloathed, thus painted, thus
ornimented, the Deliwannuck made a most terrif
- - - They held festivals at stated times which
varied in the manner of conducting them, according
to the object they had in view. At one of their
annual festivals their ceremonies were particularly
singular & different from any that were ever practised
by any nation. Here a description would give us
some idea of their religion, & would gratify the curiosity of an injenious mind.

When the time arives, which is in September, the
who whole tribe assemble. They are dressed & ornimented in the highest fashion. The women in particular have their garments & heads so adorned with
feathers, shells, & wampum, that they make a very
brilliant & grotesque appearance. The form a circle: their countanances are solemn. A Speaker
mounts a stage in the midst. At this moment two
Black Dogs led by two Boys & two white Dogs
led by two young damsels enter the circle & are
tied together. The Speaker then extended his
hands & spoke. Hail, ye favorite children of the
great and good Spirit, who resides in the Sun

who is the father of all living creatures & whose
arms encircle us all around, who defends us from
the malicious design of that great malignant Spirit
that pours upon us all the evils we endure He
gives us all our meat & our life & causes the
corn & the fruits to spring up & makes us to rejoice
in his goodness.  He hath prepared a delightful
Country to receive us, if we are valiant in battle or
are benevolent & good.  There we can pick all
kinds of delicious fruit, & have game & fish in
abundance & our women being improved in beauty
& sprightliness will cause our hearts to dance with
delight.  But wo unto you wicked, malicious mis-
chievous mortals.  Your lot will be cast in a dark
dreary, mirey swamp, where the malignant Spirit
will torment you with musquetoes & serpents & will
give you nothing to eat but toads, frogs & snails.
But my dear friends, all hail, here is a custom
which is sanctioned by time immemorial.  Look
steadfastly on the black dogs & let not your eyes
be turned away, when they are thrown on the
sacred pile & the flames are furiously consuming
their bodies, then let your earnest prayer assend
for pardon & your transgressions will flee away
like shadows & your sins will be carried by the
smoke into the shades of oblivion.  When this solemn expiatory sacrifice is ended, then prepare your
souls to partake of the holy festival Each one will
receive a precious morsel from these immaculate
snow colored dogs, in token that your offences have
all evaporated in the smoke of the holy sacrifice.
& that you are thankful to him the benevolent

Spirit, for the abundance of good things that you enjoy, & that you humbly anticipate the continuance of his blessing that he will defend you against the evil designs of that malignant Spirit, who gives us gawl & wormwood, & fills our bosom with pain & our eyes with tears. He then proclaimed, let the sacred pile be erected & the solemn sacrifice performed. Instantly about one hundred men come forward with small dry wood & bundles of dry sticks & having thrown them in one pile within the circle, they set the pile on fire. The black dogs were knocked on the middle head, & thrown on the top, in a moment all was in a blaze & the flames assended in curls to heaven. The whole company assumed the most devout attitude & muttered in sounds almost inarticulate their humble confession & earnest requests.

When the dogs were consumed & the fire nearly extinguished, the ceremonies of their sacred festival began. The white dogs which were very plump & fat were knocked on the head & their throats cut. Their hair was then singed off, having first their entrails taken out, & being suspended by the nose before a hot fire, they were soon roasted, thrown upon a long table & desected into as many pieces as there were persons to swallow them. The company immediately formed a procession, one rank of men the other of women, the men marching to the left & the women to the right of the table, each one took a piece & devoured it with as good a - - - if it had been the most delicious morsel. Having completed these sacred ceremonies with great solemnity, the whole company formed themselves into a compact circle round the stage ten musitians immediately mounted, & facing the multitude on every side sang a song. The tune & the musical voices of the singers pleased the ear, whilst the imagination was delighted with the poetic inginuity of the composition. The multitude all joined in the chorus with voice so loud & multifarious, that the atmosphere quaked with terror, & woods & neighbouring hills sent back by way of mockery, sent back the sound of their voices, their vociferation improved by ten-fold confusion. Perhaps, reader, you have the curiosity to hear the song. I can give you only the last stanzy & the chorus.

"For us the sun emits his rais
"The moon shines forth for our delight.
"The stars shine forth extol our heroes prais
"And warriors flee before our sight.

CHORUS.

"Delawan to chakee poloo
"Manegengo forwah toloo
"Chanepant, lawango chapah
"Quinebogan hamboo gowah.

The solemnities are ended & in their opinion their poor souls are compleatly whitewashed & every stain entirely effaced. A little - - - will now dissipate the solemnity & inspire them with cheerfulness & meriment. The whole tribe repair to the top of an hill, at one place their is a gradual slope a small distance, & then it desends about twenty-five feet in an almost perpendicular direction, at the bottom of which is a quagmire which is about ten feet in length.

& the soft mud is about three feet deep. At each
end the ground is soft, but not miry. Down this
declivity twenty pair of very suple & sprightly young
men & women are to desend. If by their dexterity
& agility they escape the quagmire, a piece of wampum will be the reward of each fortunate champion;
but if they plunge in their recompense will be the
ridicule of the multitude. In making this desent, six
young women & five young men by a surprizing
dexterity in whirling their bodies as they desended,
cleared themselves from the quagmire. The rest as
their turn came, plunged in & came out most wofully
muded to the great diversion of the Spectators. The
incident which excited the most meriment, hapned
when the last pair desended. by an unlucky spring to
clear himself from the quagmire he bro't his body
alongside of the declivity & roled his whole length
into the midst of the quagmire, where he lay his
whole length in an horizontal position on his back
neither heels nor head up, but horizontally, soft &
easy, but alas, when one unlucky event happens
another follows close on its heals. the fair-plump
corpulent damsel his affectionate sweetheart came
instantly sliding with great velocity. She saw the
woful position of her beloved. She wished him no
harm, she raised her feet, this bro't the center of
gravity directly over the center of his head, here she
rested a moment, his head sunk, she sunk after him,
his heels kicked against the wind like Jeshuran
waxed fat, but not a word from his lips, but his ideas
came in quick succession, tho't he, what a disgrace
to die here in the mud under the pressure of my

sweet heart, however his time for such reflections were short, the tender hearted maid collecting all her agility in one effort, dismounted & found herself on dry land in an instant, not a moment to be lost. She seized her lover by one leg, & draged him from the mud, a curious figure extending about six feet six inches on the ground, all besmeared from head to foot, spitting, puffing, panting & struggling for breath. Poor man, the whole multitude laughing at thy calamity, shouting ridiculing, none to give thee consolation but thy loving & sympathetic partner in misfortune.

Upon my soul, exclaims Droll Tom, Stern foremost. That bouncing Lass ought to have the highest prize for draging her ship from the mud. She was clean-ing the filth from his face.

## CHAPT. IV.

### A JOURNEY TO THE N. W. & REMOVALL

Gracious God! how deplorable our situation Are we doomed to dwell among hordes of savages & be deprived of all intercourse with friends & the civilized world? & what will be the situation of our offspring? Will they preserve our customs & manners, cultivate the arts & sciences & maintain our holy religion; or rather will they not rather degenerate into savages & by mingling with them become the most - - - race of beings in existence. Who can indure such reflec-tion, such heart-rending anticipation? They pour upon my soul like a flood & bear me down with the weight of a milstone. O that my head were water, &

my eyes a .fountain of tears, Then my intolerable
burthen should should be poured forth in a torrent &
my soul set at liberty.  But behold the light springs
up & beams upon my soul.  She brings in her train
Hope that celestial Godes, that sure & strong anchor
that dispenser of comfort & pleasing anticipation, &
that dispeller of corroding grief & blank dispair.  She
bids me review the exploded reasoning of of a great
philosopher & compare it with my own observations,
perhaps the result will point out a safe road to the
land of our nativity.

Thus I reasoned respecting the solar system of
which the earth is a part.  Provided the earth is stationary according to the present system of philosophy, then the sun the moon & the plannets, being at
an immense distance from the earth, must perform
their revolutions around her with inconceivable
velocity; Whereas, if according to the platonic system, the earth is a globe & the sun is stationary, then
the earth by a moderate velocity - - - perform her
revolutions.  This scheme will represent the solar
system as displaying the transendant wisdom of its
Almighty architect, for in this we behold the Sun
suspended by Onmipotence & all the plannets moving
round him as their common center in exact order &
harmony.  In this we can easily account for days &
nights & the diferent seasons of the year.  When the
earth presents one part of her face to the sun it is
day, & when that part is turned from his beams it is
night.  When she varies to the South the sun shines
upon us in a more perpendicular direction, the sun
beams become more dense & the heat increases, as

she turns back the heat decreases in proportion as this part of the earth looses its perpendicular direction, & to the sun & the cold becomes more intense in the same proportion. This account for the various seasons of the year appears correct & consistent & highly honourable to the divine perfection.

But behold the other system. The earth firmly fixed on a firm foundation, perhaps a stone, some say on a giants back who stands on a - - - back. Its surface widely extends nearly horizontal, & its cut down & its sides cut down strait or perpendicular to the the very bottom, below which is a fathomless abiss. Pray, Mr. Philosopher, what man was ever there & looked down & what prevents the Ocean, unless it is damd with earth & rocks, from pouring down & loosing itself in this horrible abis? But how exrensive is this teraqueous surface? Indeed I am of opinion if this system is true, I am nearly at one end of it. But the hipothises is too absurd & inconsistent. The earth must be of a spherical form & a westerly course will lead us to the land of our nativity. Perhaps this is a part of the eastern continent, or perhaps only a narrow strip of the Ocean intervenes? On no other principle can we account for the emigration of the ancestors of these innumerable hords of human beings that possess this continent. Their tradition is that their ancestors came from the west, & they agree in their information that at the distance of fifteen days journey in a westernly direction there

are nations vastly more numerous, powerful & civilized than themselves.

The earth therefore must be of a spherical form
a Globe & a westerly course will lead us to the land
of our nativity. On what principle can we account
for emigration of the ancestors of these innumerable hords of human beings that possess this
Continent? Their tradition tells them that they emi-
grated from the westward. From this I draw the
conclusion that the sea if any, which intervenes
between the two Continents at the westward is not
so extensive but that it may be safely navigated
I have also learnt from some of the natives We
are also informed by some of the natives that at
the distance of about fifteen days journey in a
north westerly course there is a great river which
runs in a south westerly direction, they can not tell
how far & that along the banks of this river there
are great towns & mighty kings & a people who
live in a state of civilation. From all these con-
siderations I am determined to remove, pursue a
westerly course, & seek the delightful country of my
ancestors. I immediately communicated my determination & the reasons on which it was founded to
our little Society, who joyfully acquiessed. It was
thot to be the most prudential to find out the disposition & character of the inhabitants, who were
settled along the great River lest we should fall into
the hands of Robbers. For this purpose my man
Crito & myself & a Delawan for an interpreter set
forth. We passed thro' a country interspersed with

vilages, inhabited by the same kind of people as
the Delawans, until we came to a great Mountain.
Having passed over this, we had not traveled far
before we came to the confluence of two great rivers
which in conjunction produced a river which was
called Owaho, deep enough for the navigation of
ships. Here was a lagge town or city inhabited by
a different race of people from any we had seen
before. We were immediately conducted to the King
& were received who received us very graciously,
& having asked a number of very pertinent ques-
tions & received answer to his satisfaction, I then
made known to him our business & had all my
requests granted. As we proposed to move into his
territory, he offered to furnish us for our convenience, with four Mammoons & four men to manage
them. These were an animal of prodigious magnitude even biger than the elephant, which the
natives had tamed & domesticated. They were very
sagacious & docile & were employed in carying
burthens & in drawing timber & in plowing their
land. Their hair at the Spring season was about
seven inches in length, & was of a fine wooly consistence, & being sheared off at the proper season,
was manufactured into course cloath. And the milk
of the female which they produced in abundance,
afforded a very wholesome nutriment. Having thus
succeeded beyond our expectations, we made as
much expidition to return as possible. We arrived
in safety without any material accidents. The Little Society I had left were greatly rejoiced at our
returne, & highly pleased with the account we gave

of the country we had visited, & at the sight of
those extraordinary & prodigious animals Mammoons
which we had bro't to convey our baggage. No
time was lost to make preparation for the journey.
The Captain, Mate & myself went to the King & held
a conference with him & the chiefs & obtained leave
to depart, tho' with apparent regret & reluctance.
Sacks were provided from course cloth to receive
the most valuable part of our goods & furniture.
These were thrown across three of the Mammoons
The other was caparisoned in a manner too tedious
to describe for the accommodation of our women &
children. They were all mounted upon him & rode
with great convenience & safety. Being thus prepared & ready Thus having resided among the Deli-
wans two years, & being prepared to take our departure. The King & his chiefs & many of his principal
Subjects came forward to take an affectionate fare-
well. This was done on both sides with with mutual
expressions of the most ardent & sincere friendship
& the most earnest wishes & prayers for future prosperity & happiness. Having taken our final adieu I
observed honest Crito sheding tears very plentifully. You seem to be affected, said I. God bless
your honour said he, when I think how kind & generous these poor Delawans have been to us, I can
not help feeling an affection & friendship for them.
We were obliged to anchor amongst them, we were
strangers, & helpless, & they were ignorant Savages,
yet they held out the hand of kindness, & treated
us as brothers & sisters. Have they not fulfilld the
law of Christian charity? O that they were good

Christians, may God forgive their ignorance & unbelief, & reward them for their kindness & genosity. We passed on. No obsticles impeded our journey until we came to the great river Suscowan, which lies, runs between the Deliwah River & the great moun mountain. The water being too deep for fording, we built a small boat, & with this at several times, we conveyed the whole of the baggage & company & baggage across, except the managers of the Mammoons, who mounted them & forded & swam across. We then proceeded on by slow marches. - - - But in crossing the great mountain we had some difficulties to encounter, but however met with received no material damage. but finally arived safely at the great city Owkahon on the twenty-fifth day after our departure from Delawan.

Fatigued with a long & difficult journey great joy & gladness were visible in every in countanance & all were disposed to establish our residence here, until further information could be obtained, & further measures concerted to prosecute our journey to Europe. The King & his principal officers proffered us every assistance necessary to make our situation agreeable. They assigned us in compliance with our request conformity to our desire a number of houses on the bank of the river a little distance from the city. We made him some valuable presents in return, which he received as a token of friendship, but not as a compensation. For such was the high sense of honour which this prince sustained, that when he made a present he would take it as an insult to offer him anything as a compensation.

Having now once more become settled our little community continued the same regulations which they had established at Deliwan & all things proceeded in peace & our affairs prospered.

## CHAP. V.

### A DESCRIPTION OF THE OHONS, & MANNER OF PROCURING A LIVING.

I AM now to describe a species of nation who have but little resemblance to those to those inumerable tribes of savages, who live along the coast of the Atlantic. Their complexion, the form & construction of their bodies, their customs manners laws government & religion all demonstrate that they must have originated from some other nation & have but a very distant affinity with their savage neighbors. As to their persons they were taller on an average than I had ever seen in any nation, their bones were large limbs strait & shoulders broad. Their eyes rather smalll & sunk deep in the head. Their foreheads were prominent & the face below tapering in such a manner that the chin that was formed nearly to a point. As to their complexion it was bordering on an olive tho' of a lighter shade. Their eyes were generally of a dark brown or black. Their hair of the same color, tho' I have sometimes seen persons, whose hair was of a redish hue.

They cloathed themselves in choath which was manufactured among themselves from the hair of the Mammoon & from Cotton, which was transported from the South west westward. The men wore shoes

& long stockings wide trouses, a waistcoat & a garment with wide short sleaves, which came down to their nees, & in cold weather a cloak over the whole. The covering for the head was generaly a kind of a Cap, which ran up high & tapered to a point. This was generally made of fur skins & was ornimented with feathers. It had a small brim in the shape of an half moon to project over the forehead. The women besides stockings & shoes wore a short petecoat a shirt of cotton a loose garment with sleaves which they girted round them with belts & a cloack. They had various orniments such as ribbons made from cotton & coulared with different coulars, the most beautiful feathers that could be obtained & shells of various kinds. Indeed the higher class of women were extremely fond of ornament, & wore placed a large share of their happiness in the brilliancy & gaudy appearance of their garments. These people obtained their living generally by the cultivation of the Land, & the manage by tending & managing certain animals which had been so long domesticated that they had lost their wild nature & become tame. Corn, wheat, beans, squashes & carrots they raised in great abundance. The ground was plowed by horses & generally made very mellow for the reception of the seed.

It was the occupation of a certain part of the men to tend upon the tame animals, to drive them to pasture, & keep them from straying, & feed them when the snow was on the ground. Two men would tend twenty Mammouth, which were indifferent whether they fed on grass or cropt the bushes. When these

animals were fat their flesh was highly esteemed.
They had droves of Elk, which they had so tamed
& tutored that they could manage them as they
pleased.   These had their tenders (several words
illegible) & would follow them like a flock of
of sheep.   & it was but seldom that any would leave
their companions.   The elk constituted a considerable portion of their animal food.   The horses were
managed in the same way & the people tho't their
meat to be a savoury dish.   They had large numbers
of turkies & gees, which tho' originally wild, yet by
treating them with great familiarity by croping their
wings & feeding them they frequently they discovered
no disposition to ramble off, but would propogated
their species & laid eggs in abundance.

Hunting & fishing were the employment of some
others followed the mechanical buciness & others carried on a bartering trade to the Southwestward in order
to furnish to furnish the people with cotton & other articles whose production was not congenial to their cli-
mate.   By pursuing these various employments they
generally had an abundance of provision & were at
all seasons comfortably cloathed.   And here I would
remark as one striking characteristic of this people,
that they observed great neatness in their dress, in
their cookery & in their houses.

The manufacturing of lead Iron & lead was under-
stood, but was not carried on to that extent & perfection as in Europe.   A small quantity of Iron in
proportion to the number of Inhabitants served to
supply them with all the impliments which custom

had made necessary for their use. By hammering & hardening their Iron they would convert it nearly into the consistence of Steal & fit it for the purpose of edged tools.

The potery business was conducted with great inginuity & great quantities of stone & earthen ware consisting of every kind of vessel of every construction which were needed for family use, were manufactured in every part of this extensive country. They would These vessels they they orniminted with pictures with the likenessess of various kinds of animals & trees & impressed upon them such coulars as would strike the fancy with delight. The females of the high Class most welthy Class would often have a large & superfluous quantity of this brittle furniture tò decorate one apartment of the house. The vessels they arranged in such order as to make a display of taste & impress the mind with the agreeable sensation of beauty.

In Architecture there can be no comparison with the civilized nations of Europe. In their most welthy and populous Cities they their houses & public buildings exhibit no eligance, no appearance of wealth or grandure, all is plain & nothing superfluous. But convenience seems to be the whole object they had in view in the construction of their buildings of every kind.

Their houses were generally but one story high built of wood, being framed & covered with split clapboards or shingles, & in the inside the walls were formed of clay, which was plastered over with a thin coat of lime. Their houses seldom consisted of more than three apartments. As to their chimneys they built construct a wall of stone about five feet hight for the fire to be against which they build their fire, from the top of this wall they construct the chimney with thin pieces of split timber, on the inside with wet dirt or clay of which they plaister wet dirt or clay which compleatly covers & adheres to the timber & prevents the fire from having any operation upon it. The inside of their houses as the women generally practise neatness, makes a much better appearance than the outside.

It is my opinion says Trojanus that this people display a taste in building which is formed upon the true principles of Reason. Their houses are sufficiently spacious for convenience. No expense or Labour are thrown away in building useless apartments or in erecting their houses higher than what convenience requires. The whole catalogue of ornamental trumpery is neglected. This in Rome produces more than half the Labour & expense in building. Yes says Lucian, and without this these labouring people must starve for want of employment, & the citizens of the Roman empire would be deprived of the honour of possessing a splendid Capital & of the exquisite pleasure of beholding the greatest exhibition of human ingenuity in the elegance the splendour the purity & beauty of their houses, their palaces & their public edifices. True indeed, replies Trojanus, men may be dazed & delighted with such objects for the moment, But could not wealth be better bestowed upon to promote interest of the community & for charitable purposes & these artists better employ their strength & ingenuity in producing some substantial benefits to themselves & others? Rejoins Lucian, the course reason dictates is to avoid extremes. A slab coulared world would tire the senses by its uniformity & too much orniment & splendor, would cease to please by its frequency.

Besides, lofty houses can be more easily overthrown by tornadoes or tumbled down upon our heads by earthquakes. The course, says Lucian that reason dictates is to avoid extremes. A slab coulored world by its uniformity would tire the senses, & by its possessing too much ornament & splendor it would cease to please. (But the wonder wont cease when it is considered that mankind with but few exceptions to walk in the tracks of their fathers & to pursue the road marked out by their education.)

## CHAP. VI.

### DESCRIPTION OF THE LEARNING, RELIGION & CUSTOMS OF THE OHONS.

LEARNING appears to be so important to the nature of man & a good convenient share of it so easy to obtain, that some may wonder why it is not universally diffused thro' the world. But If we can place any reliance on the dark annals of antient history, it is certain that letters are indebted for their existence to the inventive genius of certain extraordinary characters. Egypt & Chaldea contended for the honour of being the first who invented letters. Perhaps they were invented in each nation nearly at the same time. But let this be as it may could no other nation in the world produce as great geniuses as Egypt or Chaldea?* Is there any natural obsticle to prevent their production in America as well as in Asia? Whatever may be the reasoning of some on this subject, the fact is that I found Letters or some share of learning, tho' in a very imperfect state among this people. At present I shall wave the account of its introduction & shall merely describe the state of learning as it existed among the Ohons. They had characters which represent words & all compound words were had each part represented by its appropriate character. The variation of cases, moods & tenses was designated by certain marks placed under the characters. They generally wrote on parchment & beginning at the right wrote from the top to the bottom, placing each character directly under the preceeding one & having finished one column or line they begin the write the next on the left of that & so continue on until they cover the parchment if the subject requires it. It is a work of considerable labour & time to obtain such a knowledge of their characters & the application as to be able to read with fluencey & to write with ease & accuracy.

In the principal Cities & towns the government appointed learned men to instruct the sons of the

---

* Note. The most probable conjecture is that they were communicated from one nation to the other.

higher class of Citizens & in the course of four or five
years they will make such proficiency as to become
tolerable schollars.

The works of the learned are not very voluminous.
Records are kept of the transactions of their government. Their constitution & laws are committed to
writing. A sacred Roll in manuscript is preserved
among the Records of their Emporors & kings. & are
dispersed thro' the Empire & much pains taken to
diffuse the knowledge of them among the people. In
all their large towns & Cities they have deposited
under the care of a priest a sacred Roll which contains the tenets of their Theology & a description of
their religious ceremonies. This order of men publish comments upon these sacred writings. They
publish some tracts on moral philosophy & some containing a collection of proverbs & the wise sayings
of their sages.

But the kind of composition in which they most
exult is poetry. In poetic numbers they describe
the great events which take place & the exploits &
mighty achievements of their heroes. In soft elegies
they describe paint the Amours of Lovers & in
pathetic strains they delineate the calamities of sorrow of the unfortunate.

In their assemblies it is very common for a certain
class of these learned poets to entertain the company
(- - - line gone - - - -) with a resital of poetic
pieces describing the batles & exploits of their warriors, or to sing some amourous or witty ballad. As
for theators they have none, but as a kind of sussti-
tute there are actors who entertain the people by

pronounsing dialogues or plays in which they display
all the arts of mimicry & act out the express in their
countanance their gesture & the tone of their voices
the different passions of the human mind.   As only
a small portion of the people are instructed in the
arts of reading & writing, of consequence the great
mass must possess a large share of ignorance, but
not so great a share as savages who have no learning among them.   They hear the conversation & the
lectures of their sages, they are entertained with Their
poetic orators entertain them with the productions
of their poets, containing the history of great events
& mighty athievements.   Their actors divert & please
them by exciting the various passions at the same
time communicating instruction & correcting the natural savageness of manner by & as the pieces they
rehearse contain many ideas & sentiments tending to
expose the deformity of vice & the folly of superstition & the disgustingness of rude & clownish manners, the people are of consequence improved &
considerably refined & add to their living in compact
towns or considerable cities in which there is a constant & reciprocal communication of ideas, which of
course would have no small effect to inform their
minds.   To all these causes combined the Ohons the
great mass of the people are indebted for possessing
a considerable share of knowledge & civilization.

## RELION VII.

IN every nation there is some kind of Religion & in every religion, however adulterated & corrupted, there are some things which are commendable, some things which serve to improve the morals & influence mankind to conduct better than what they would do provided they pursued the natural dictates of their depraved mind. <u>without any restraint</u> As this sentiment is an established maxim which has been believed in every nation from the earliest ages <u>in every nation</u>, hense it has been the policy of all governments to encourage & protect some kind of religion. In examining the religious systems, sentiments & precepts which are believed & practised throughout this extensive Empire, & which are encouraged & protected by the government. I found some things which are common to the various systems of theology in Europe & Asia, & some things which have no resemblance to either From the sacred Roll as it is denominated I shall extract the tenets of their theology & a description of their religious ceremonies. It expresses them them to this effect

"There is an intelligent omnipotent Being who is self-existent & infinitely good & benevolent. Matter eternally existed. He put forth his hand & formed it into such bodies as he pleased. He presides over the universe & has a perfect knowledge of all things. From his own spiritual substance he formed seven . sons. These are his principal agents to manage the affairs of his empire.  He formed the bodies of men from matter.  Into each body he <u>emitted</u> infussed a particle of his own spiritual substance, in consequence of which man in his first formation was inclined to benevolence & goodness.  There is also another great intelligent Being who is self-existent & possessed of great power but not of Omnipotence.  He is filled with infinite malice against the good Being & exerts all his subtlety & power to ruin his works.  Seing the happy situation of man he approached so near as to tuch his soul with his deliterious hand.  The poison was immediately diffused & contaminated his passions & appetites.  His reason & understanding received no injury.  The good being looking upon his unhappy offspring with infinite love & compassion, made a decree that if mankind would reduce their passions & appetites under the government of reason, he should <u>be</u> enjoy blessings in this world, & be compleatly happy after <u>death</u> his soul quits his body.  Death dissolves the connection.  Material Bodies are prepared for the souls of the righteous.  These bodies can pass thro' any part of the universe & are invisible to mortal eyes.  Their place of residence is on a <u>great & city</u> vast plain, which is beautiful with magnificent buildings, with Trees fruits & flowers.  <u>Here they enjoy</u> <u>every delight which</u> No imagination can paint the delights the felicity of the Righteous.  But the wicked <u>have no etherial</u> are denied etherial bodies.  Their souls naked & incapable of seeing light dwel in darkness & are tormented with the keenest anguish.

Ages roll away & the good Being has compassion upon them. He permits them to take possession of etherial bodies & they arise quick to the abodes of delight & glory. Now, O man, attend to thy duty & thou shalt escape the portion of the wicked. & enjoy all the delights of the righteous. Avoid all acts of cruelty to man & beast.*

defraud not thy neighbours nor suffer thy hands secretly to convey his property from him. Preserve thy body from the contamination of lust, & remember that the seduction of thy neighbours wife would be a great Crime. Let thy citizens be numbered once in two years, & if the young women who are fit for marriage are more numerous than the young men, then wealthy men who are young & who have but one wife shall have the privilege with the permission of the king to marry another until the number of the single young women & the single young men are made equal. But he who hath two wives shall have a house provided for each & he shall spend his time equally with each one.

Be grateful for all favours & forsake not thy friend in adversity. Treat with kindness & reverence thy Parents. Forsake them not in old age nor let their cheek be furrowed with tears for the want of bread. Bow down thy head before the aged, treat thy superiors with respect, & place thy rulers & thy teachers in the most honourable seats. Let Rulers consult the welfare of the people & not agrandize themselves by

*No crime is so horrid as maliciously to destroy the life of man.

oppression & base bribes. Let Religious Teachers walk in the road which leads to celestial happiness & lead the people after them. Let Parents restrain the vices of their children & instruct their minds in useful knowledge. Contention & Strife is is the Bane of Families & the destruction of domestick happiness, being yoked together the husband & wife ought to draw in the same direction. Their countanances will then appear beautiful shine with the effulgent Beams of Friendship & love, peace & harmony will attend their habitation & their affairs will prosper.

Hold out the hand of kindness & friendship to thy neighbour, consider him when reduced to indigence & distress, He is as dear to the great & good being as what thou art. & thou now hast an opportunity to manifest the disposition of thy heart To afford him relief will be pleasing to thy Maker & an expression of thy gratituge.

Envious & malicious Souls are almost incurably contaminated with that hellish poison which which was first disordered the soul of man. Partake not of their guilt by joining them in the malignant work of slander & detraction. Their intended mischief returns upon their own heads, & the slandered character of the innocent & just shines forth with increasing lustre. Let the stranger find an hospitable resting place under thy roof. Give him to eat from thy portion that when he departs he may bless thee & go on his way rejoicing.

Industry will Say not to thyself I will indulge inactivity & idleness & lie upon the bed of sloth &

slumber away the precious moments of time, for in this thou art unwise, for unwise disease will attend thee, hunger will torment thee & Rags will be thy clothing. Let industry & economy fill up the measure of thy waking moments. So shall thy countanance display health & sprightliness, plenty shall supply the wants of thy family & thy reputation shall be respectable.

But behold a being in human form from whom I turn away in disgust & abhorrence. He is covered with so much dirt & filth that no etherial body is provided for him nor can he be received into the abodes of the blessed. Suffer not thy bodies or thy garments to remain long besmeared with dirt & filth. Cleanliness prevents many diseases & is pleasant to the sight. But from a dirty filthy mortal we turn with disgust & abhorrance. As the great Author of our existence being is benevolent to all his offspring, so it becomes us to be benevolent to our fellow beings around us. Oou Country is one body & we are part of its members. We are therefore bound to maintain their rights & priviledges & the the honour & dignity of our Country at the risk of our lives. Great rewards attend the brave & their exploits & achievements in contending against tyrants & in defending the Rights their of their Country will be celebrated on the plains. But the vision now expands & directs our contemplation to fix on his attributes, whose spiritual substance is commensurate with infinity. As only a single particle from his substance constitutes our souls, how small how diminutive must we

appear in the view of Omniscience. We must therefore contemplate his attributes thro' the medium of
his works, & admire with profound reverance &
adoration his wisdom goodness & power which are
visible in the formation & arrangement of all material
bodies & spiritual beings. He requires us to supli-
cate his favours, & when received to express our
gratitude. As our passions & appetites often get the
assendence of our reason, we are therefore bound to
confess our faults & implore forgiveness.

Now that you may know and keep all these thing
which were made known by divine inspiration, it is
ordained that on every eighth day, ye lay aside all
unnecessary labour, that ye meet in convenient
numbers & form assemblies, that at each assembly
a learned holy man shall preside, who shall lead your
devotions & explain this sacred Roll & give you such
instruction as shall promote your happiness in this
life & in the life to come. Once in three months ye
shall hold a great festival in every great city & town,
& your priests shall sacrifice an Elk as a token that
your sins deserve punishment, but that the divine
mercy hath banished them into shades of forgetful-
ness.

Be attentive oh man, to the words of truth which
have been recorded & & respect to all the command-
ments which have been written for your observance.
Your Maker will then be rejoiced to see you rejoice
in the participation of his favour & to behold your
faces brighten with the cheering benign beams of
cheerfulness.

AN ACCOUNT OF BASKA CHAP VIII

AMONG the great & illustrious characters who have appeared in the world in different ages as instructors & reformers of mankind, Baska holds is entitled to a conspicuous place.

The place of his nativity is not recorded. But the first notice which is given of him is his appearing at the great City of Golanga, which is situate on the Banks of the Siota River. He was attended by his wife & two little sons. The fashion of their garments were different from the natives. Their complexion likewise was of a little whiter. They were Baska was grave solemn & sedate reserved in his conversation, 'but when he spoke wisdom proceeded from his lips. His fame spread rapidly thro' the city & country, & he was celebrated as a man of the most brilliant & extraordinary talents. He was conducted to the King & introduced to him. The King asked him from what country he came. His reply was, at a great distance from the westward. He then asked·him induced him to come into his country. He replied

- - - - - - - - - - - - - - - - - -


## CHAPT VIII

PERHAPS reader, before we describe the government of the Ohons it might be proper to relax our mind by with a few sceches of Biography. The character which will best connect with the history of the learning & religion & the government & laws of the Ohons is that of the great and illustrious Lobaska.

He is the man who first introduced their present method of writing who presented them with the sacred Roll which contains the tenets & precepts of their religion, & who formed their political constitution as it respects the connection of various kingdoms or tribes under one government.

There are many anecdotes which tradition has handed down respecting this extraordinary man, which have the complexion of fables the miraculous & hence I conclude they must be fabulous Such as his As for instance he is represented as forming a curious machine by which & having placed himself upon it he mounted into the Atmosphere & assended a great hight & having sailed a considerable time distance thro' the air he desended slowly & received no damage & that multitudes of astonished Spectators had a number of times seen him perform this miraculous exploit, & that he declared that when he took these excursions, his extraordinary wisdom & knowledge was communicated to him. If he did in fact perform such exploits no wonder that he managed an ignorant people as he pleased. But as it is not my intention to amuse my readers by a splendid relation of fables, I shall confine myself to facts which cannot be contested. The place of his nativity is not recorded. The first account given of him was his appearance in the great City of Golanga which is situate on the Banks of the Siota River. When he entered that city he was attended by his wife & four sons the the eldest of whom was about eighteen years of age. He himself appeared to be about forty. His

personal appearance was commanding being of mid-
ling Stature of a bold frank countanance & eyes lively
& penetrating. In his general deportment he was
cheerful yet displayed much sedateness & gravity.
He was affable & familiar in conversation but not
loquacious, he never would converse long on trifling
subjects, had a wonderful faculty to intermix some
wise sayings & remarks that should improve & of
turning with dignity and gravefulness the attention
of the company to subjects that were important &
interesting. None could then withstand the energy
of his reasoning, & all were astonished at the ingenuity of his arguments & the great knowledge &
wisdom which he displayed. His fame spread thro'
the City & multi & country & multitudes frequently
assembled & importuned him to give them instruction.
Always cheerful to gratify the curiosity & comply
with the reasonable requests of the multitude, he
entertained them by conversing with them familiarly,
& by exhibiting public discourses. All were charmed
with his wisdom & eloquence, and all united in pro-
nouncing him to be the most extraordinary man in
existence, & generally believed that he had conversation with the celestial beings, & always acted under
the influence of divine inspiration. The people were
very liberal in their donations, which enabled him to
support his family in affluence. Having thus in a
short time established a character with respect to
wisdom & eloquence to any man who had ever
appeared before him in the nation, he then at an
enterview which he held with the king & the chiefs
told them that he had invented the art of expressing

ideas by certain marks or characters, & having explained the nature of the subject to their full satisfaction, he then proposed to establish a school for the instruction of the sons of the principal subjects of the King. This proposal was received & accepted with much gratitude & cheerfulness. A house was immediately prepared for the accommodation of Schollars, & in a short time the number amounted to nearly two hundred. But here it must be observed that the art of making & applying the characters to the words which they represented, was taught principally by his sons. They had all received an education from their father & even the youngest who was but eleven years old could read & write with great correctness. & facility. He superintended their instruction & very frequently gave them lectures on scientific & moral subjects, his schollars made great progress in learning & delighted their parents with the improvement they had made in literature civilization & refinement. He still continued to associate among the people, & was indefatigable in his labours to dispel their ignorance, correct their superstition & vices & to diffuse a more accurate knowledge of the mechanical arts. The manufacture of Iron in particular was not known. This he taught a number by showing them how to build a small furnace, & to cast iron ware, & then to build a small forge & there refine pigs, & convert them into Iron.

He had resided among the Siotans about three years, & the happy effects of his labours were visible to all observers. A great reformation had taken place in the morals & manners of the people, Industry had encreased, & agriculture & the mechanical arts had received great improvement & houses were built on a more commodious & eligant construction. But not willing to stop here the benevolent mind of the great Tobaska meditated a more important revolution. Now was the propitious era to had arived & the way was prepared for the introduction of that system of Theology, which is comprized in the sacred Roll.

In the first place he read & explained the whole system to the King & the chiefs of the nation, who cordially gave it their approbation & gave permission to propogate it among the people. Under the pretense that this system was revealed to him in several enterviews, which he had been permitted to have with the second son of the great & good Being, the people did not long hesitate but received as sacred & divine truth every word which he taught them. They forgot their old religion which was a confused & absurd medly of Idolitry & superstitious nonsense & embraced a religion more sublime & consistent, & more fraught with sentiments which would promote the happiness of mankind in this world.

Whilst the Siotans were thus rapidly progressing in their improvements they were unhappily disturbed by the certain prospect of war. Bombal, the King of the Kentucks, a nation that lived on the south side of the great River Ohio, had taken great umbrage against Kadokam the King of Siota. This Bombal was the most haughty & the most powerful prince who reigned in this part of the western Continent. It had been the custom for several ages for the King

& chiefs of the Kentucks to have the exclusive right to wear in their caps a bunch of blue feathers, which designated their preeminence over every nation. The Siotan princes envying them this distinguished honor & considering themselves as being at least their equals assumed the liberty to place bunches of Blue feathers upon their caps. This in the opinion of the Kentucks was an unpardonable offense if persisted in, & a most daring insult upon their supreme dignity. A messenger was immedi After a solemn Council was held with his chiefs Bombal, with their unanimous consent dispatched a messenger to Kadocam, who thus proclaimed.

Thus saith Bombal, the king of kings & the most mighty prince on earth. Ye have insulted my our honour & dignity, in assuming blue feathers which was the badge of our preeminence. Know ye that uless you tear them from your caps ye shall feel the weight of our ven-gence.

Kadocam replied. Tell your master that a great Company of Wolves made an attack upon a City, to rob the citizens of their dear & elk, & they let forth their dogs upon them, which attacked them with such fury, & courage that they fled mangled & torn to a most dreary swamp. Here they by the most tremendous the most plaintive howling, they lamented their sad disaster & disgrace.

An answer so shrewd & insulting it was expected would soon be followed by an invasion. Measures must immediately be taken for the defense of the kingdom. Lobaska was invited to set in council. All

were unanimously of opinion that to comply with the
haughty demand of Bombal, by tearing the Blue
feathers from their caps would be degrading the
honour of the nation & a relinquishment of their
natural right, that they were likewise sensible that
the most vigorous exertions were necessary to save
the country from ruin. The opinion & advice of
Lobaska was requested. It is my opinion says he
that by using a little stratigem, this war might be
bro't to a conclusion. which will be honourable to this
kingdom. We will pursue, says the King your
advice & directions. I shall be happy says Lobaska
to assist you with my best advice. Call immediately
into the field an army of three Thousand men, provide two thousand shovels five hundred mathooks &
five hundred wheelbarrows, & one hundred axes. I
will give directions how to make them. Not a
moment was lost. The army was assembled, & impliments provided with the utmost expidition. & they
marched down the river. to a certain place where the
Army of the Enimy must pass in order to arrive at
the city of Golanga. At this place the hills or moun-
tains came within less than a mile of the river, & a
flat or level land intervened. Here Lobaska directed
that a canal should be cut from the River to the River
to the Hill That it should be eight feet wide & eight
deep & that the dirt which they dug should be thrown
into the river. That the canal except what should be
wanted to lay over thin pieces of split timber, which
should be extended over the canal so weak & slender
that the weight of a man would break them down.
This novel invention invention was soon carried into

effect & the work compleatly finished. Every pre-
caution was used to prevent any intelligence of these
transactions from getting to the enimy.

In the meantime Kadokam bro't into the field seven
thousand more of his warriors, men of brave hearts &
valiant for the battle. The indignant king of the Kentucks had by this time assembled an army of Thirty
Thousand men, who were ready at the risk of their
lives to vindicate the preeminence of their nation.
& the transendent dignity of their King & his chiefs.
Had of this At the head of this army Bombal began
his march to execute his threatened vengance on the
Siotans. As he entered their country he found the
viliges deserted, & all the movable property conveyed away. not a man or wom was to be seen until
he came in view of the army of Kadokam, who
was encamped within a small distance of the Canal.
Bombal halted & formed his men in two Ranks,
extending from the River to the Hill. He had a
reserved core, who were placed in the rear of the main
body, Having thus arranged them for battle he went
from one wing to the other, proclaiming alould, we
have been insulted, brave Soldiers, by these cowardly Siotans. They have assumed the blue Feather
the badge of our preeminance & exalted dignity.
Behold it flying in their Caps. Will your highborn
souls submit to behold such Dastards place themselves on equal terms with you? No, my valiant
warriors, let us revenge the insult by the destruction of their puny army, & the conflagration of their
city. Make a furious charge upon them & & the
victory is ours. Let your motto be blue Feather &

you will fight like wolves robbed of their puppies. Hadokam had by this time formed his army in order of Battle close to the edge of the canal & extended them in one rank only from the River to the Hill. As the Kentucks approached within a small distance, the Siotans gave back & began a retreat with apparent confusion, notwithstanding the pretended efforts of the King & his officers to prevent their retreating. Bombal, observing this commanded to rush forward on the full run, but to keep their ranks in order. This they instantly obeyed as one man, & as soon as their feet stept on the slender covering of the canal it gave way & they fell to the bottom, some in one position & some in another. A disaster so novel & unexpected might have appalled the stoutest & filled their minds with amazement & terror. Nor did this compleat their misfortune of the army of Bombal. An ambush of the Siotans, who lay on the side of the hill opposite to the reserved Corps of the Kentucks, rushed down upon them in an instant. Surprize & terror prevented resistance, they threw down their arms & surrendered. The retreating army of Hadocam immediately returned with shouting to the edge of the Canal. Their enimies, who but a moment before thot themselves invincible & certain of victory, were now defenceless & wholly in their power. When Lobaska was present & saw the success of his stratigem, his great soul disdained revenge on an enimy helpless & prostrate enimy. He conjured the Siotans not to shed one drop of Blood, but to be generous & merciful. Bombal had now recovered from his

surprize, & feeling the deplorable situation of his
army, his haughty soul felt the keenest anguish.
Where says he is the King of the Siotans? Here I am
says Hadokam. What is your re-quest my brother?
Reduced says he by stratigem the most ingenious &
artful to a situation which subjects us wholly under
your power, & in which you can take ample revenge.
I now implore your generosity & compassion for my
army. Spare their lives & then name your terms, &
if I can comply with them without degrading the
honour of my crown it shall be done. Your request
says Hadokam is granted Surrender your army, & let
you army return in peace. As for your majesty &
the chiefs of your nation who are present, you will
give us the pleasure of your company in our return
to the city of Golanga, there we will execute a treaty
of peace & amity, that shall be advantageous & honourable to both nations. These terms were accepted
& the Kentucks returned in peace to their own Country, not to describe exploits & bloody victories, but
the curious stratigem of Lobaska.

The two kings & their splendid retinue of princes
having arived at Golanga, every attention was paid
by the Hodokam & his chiefs to their honorable
visitors. Hadokam made a sumptuous entertainment
at which all were present. The next day both parties
met for for the purpose of agreeing to terms of peace
& perpetual amity. What are your terms says Bombal? Lobaska, says Hadokam, shall be our Arbitrator. He shall name the terms his wisdom will dictate
nothing which will be dishonourable for either party.

Your proposal, says Bombal is generous. Lobaska shall be our Arbitrator. Lobaska then rose. Attend, says he to my words, ye princes of Siota & Kentuck. You have all derived your existence from the great Father of Spirits, you are his children & belong to his great family. Why, then have you thirsted for each others' blood? for the Blood of Brothers? & what has, & what has produced this mighty war? A blue feather, may it please your majesties, a blue feather a badge of preeminence. It is pride, it is unruled ambition & avarice which devastate the world & produce rivers of human Blood. & the wars which take place among nations generally originate from as trifling causes as the blue feather.

Let this be the first article of your treaty that any person may wear a blue feather in his Cap, or any other feather that he pleases.

Let this be the second, that the individuals of each nation may carry on a commerce with each other, & that they shall be protected in their persons & property.

Let this be the third, that I shall be at liberty to establish a school or schools in any part of the dominion of Kentuck & furnish them with such instructors as I please That none shall be restrained from hearing our instructions & that we shall be patronized & protected by the King & his chiefs.

Let this be the fourth, that perpetual peace & amity shall remain between both nations & as a pledge for the fulfilment of these articles on the part of the princes of Kentuck, that the eldest son of the King &

four sons of the principal chiefs, shall be left as hos-
tiges in this City for the term of Term of Three years.
These terms met the cordial approbation of both
parties & were ratified in the most solemn manner.

Thus happy was the termination of the war about
the blue feather having taken place Lobaska proceeded with indefatigable industry & perseverance in
his benevolent scheme of enlightening & reforming
mankind. And how happy would it be for mankind
if all wars about as trifling causes as this might terminate in the same way. The benevolent mind of
Loboska soared above trifles viewing all mankind as
brothers & sisters he wished the happiness of all. He
then made provision in the treaty with the Kentucks
for the introduction of schools in Kentuck amongst
them. This was the first step which he foresaw would
introduce improvement in agriculture & the mechanical arts, produce a reformation in their morals &
religious principals, & a happy revolution in some
part of their political institutions.

Bombal had become so captivated with Lobaska,
that he invited him to bear him company to his own
dominions. He consented, & when he had arived at
the royal City of Gamba, which is situate on the
River Kentuck, he there pursued the same course
which he had done at Golanga, & his success
answered his most sanguine expectations. The people were now prepared for the introduction of a school.
He returned back to Tolanga, & sent his second son
& three of the most forward scholars of the Siotans to
establish a school at Gamba.

In the meantime his intention was to make some amendments in the government of Sciota. But as there were several Cities & a great number of viliages that acknowledged the jurisdiction of the Sciotan king which still were ignorant of the principles & doctrines which he taught, he found it necessary to visit them & to introduce instructors amongst them. In this work he was engaged about two years, & the happy effect of his labors were now visible, in various kinds of improvement & in the reformation of manners morals & religion. The way was now prepared to introduce his system of government. The chiefs of the nation were invited to attend a grand council at Tolanga. When they were met Lobaska rose, & presented them with the following constitution of government.

The king of Siota shall be stiled the Emperor of Ohion & the King of Siota, his crown shall be hereditary in the oldest male heir of his family. The cities & vilages who acknowledge his jurisdiction or who may hereafter do it, shall be entitled to protection from the Emperor. If invaded by an enimy, he shall defend them with all the force of the Empire. Once every year, the chiefs shall meet at Golanga to make laws for the good of the nation.

These young men having imbibed the spirit & principle of their great preceptor, spared no exertions to instruct the schollars & to diffuse useful knowledge amongst the people. The happy effects of their Labors were visible in a short time. The people The people embraced the religion of Lobaska & became more industrious & civilized. In their various improvements in agriculture, the mechanical arts they & literature they even exeled the Sciotans, & appeared to be as prosperous & flourishing. Even Bombal himself declared that the termination of the war about the blue feather, which at first appeared unfortunate, yet as it occationed such happy effects among his people, it gave him more satisfaction & pleasure than the reputation of being a great Conqueror. what he could have received from the reputation of being a great Conqueror.

## CHAP. IX.

### GOVERNMENT & MONEY

THE people who were denominated Ohians were settled on both sides of the River Ohio from & along the various branches of the river. The settlements extended to a great distance in the time of Lobaska, but how far it is not mentioned. They lived in comfortable villages or towns except the cities. We might except the cities, Golanga on the River Sciota & Gamba on the which River Kentuck. The various villiges or towns formed independent soveranties, & were governed by their respective chiefs.

Excepting the Cities of Golanga & Gamba, whose Kings claimed jurisdiction over an extent of country of country of about one hundred & fifty miles along the River Ohio & about the same extent distance back from the River, the remaining part of this extensive

country was settled in compact vialiges or towns &
These formed 'independent soveranties & were governed by their respective chiefs. Frequent bicker-
ings contentions & wars took place among these
chiefs, which were often attended with perilous con-
sequences. To remedy these evils & to facilitate &
accomplish the general & benevolent plan, of reforming & civilizing the Ohians, Lobaska had formed a
system of Government, with a design of establishing
two great Empires one on each side of the River
Ohio. Their different constitutions were on the same
plan & were presented by the hand of Lobaska to the
respective Kings of Sciota & Kentuck.

The Sciotan Constitution was comprised in these
words.

The country east of the great River Ohio shall
form the Empire of Sciota. At the head of this
Empire shall be placed with the title of Emperor,
Labamack the oldest son of Lobaska. The office
shall be hereditary in the eldest male of his family.
He and his sons successively shall marry natives of
the kingdom of Sciota & all their daughters shall
marry within their own dominions. He shall have
four counsellors. He, with the advice of his counsellors, shall have the exclusive right, of making war
& peace, & of forming treaties with other nations.
He shall be the commander in chief of all the forces
of the King & the King of Sciota shall be next to him.
All controversies between the rulers or chiefs of the
different tribes shall be reffered to the decision of him
& his counsellors, & he is authorized to compel a
compliance. He shall hold his settings annually in

four different parts of the Empire. The King of Sciota & the chiefs of the different tribes shall hold their offices & exercise the same authority in civil matters that they have done. They shall be amenable to the emperor & his counsellors, whose duty it shall be to inquire into all complaints against them from their subjects & to redress grievances & punish for oppression & injustice by fines. He & his Counsellors shall have the explusive priviledge of coining money. They may likewise lay taxes for the support of the government & for the defence of the nation. They shall coin no more money than what is necessary for the convenience of the people, & in such quantity only that the value shall not depreciate. In time of war he shall appoint the officers of his army except where the chiefs chuse to command their own subjects. In that case, they shall be subject to the commands of the Emperor. The people in every City town or village shall respectively chuse one or more Censors, whose duty it shall be to enquire into all mal-conduct of rulers, & all vicious & improper conduct of the priests & the people & they shall pursue such measures to obtain justice & to preduce a reformation of morals in the offenders as the laws shall direct.

In order that the priests & instructors of learning may know & perform their duty for the benefit of civilization, morality & religion, Lambon the third son of Lobaska shall preside over them & shall have the title of high Priest, & the office shall be hereditary in the eldest males of his family successively. There shall be associated with him four priests as his assistants. They shall exercise a jurisdiction over all the priests of the Empire, & shall see that they faithfully perform the duties of their office. They shall attend to the instructors of learning & shall direct that a suitable number are provided thro'out the Empire. It shall likewise be their duty at all suitable times & places to instruct Rulers & people in the duties of their respective Stations, & to labour incessantly to persuade mankind to restrain subject their passions & appetites under the government of Reason. that they may secure happiness to themselves in this life & immortal happiness beyond the grave. The people shall make contribution in proportion to their wealth for the support of their priests. If any refuse they shall be denied the priviledge of their instructions & shall be subjected to the ridicule & contempt of the people.

For the convenience of the people and the easy support of the government it is necessary that there government shou should be something which shall represent property, & which is of small weight. It is therefore provided that certain small pieces of iron stamped in a peculiar manner shall be this circulating medium. Each piece according to its particular stamp shall have a certain value fixed upon it. It shall be the peculiar prerogative of the Emperor & his counsellors to direct the coining of these pieces, which shall be denominated money. No more money shall be coined than what will be for the benefit of the Empire, nor shall the Emperor & his counsellors receive any more of it than an adequate compensation for their services. They shall keep an

account of the amount of money coined annually &
the manner in which it has been distributed &
expended. This account shall be submitted to the
examination of the King of Sciota & the chiefs of the
Empire. The Emperor shall always be ready to
receive the petitions & complaints of his subjects.
He shall consult the welfare of his people & save
them from oppression & tyranny & by his beneficent
acts shall gain their affections & obtain the appella-
tion of a just, a good & a glorious Prince.

When Hadocam King of Sciota had received this
plan of government, he immediately assembled all the
chiefs or princes within his kingdom. Lobaska
pointed out the defects of the existing governments,
& the excellencies of that form which he presented
for their acceptance. His reasons could not be
resisted, they unanimously agreed to establish it as
their constitution of Government. Labamack
accepted the office of Emperor & his four counsellor
were appointed. Lambon was ordained high Priest &
his four assistants chosen. The new government was
now put in operation. The various tribes living con-
tiguous to the Empire seeing its prosperity, solicited
the priviledge of being received as parts of the
Empire. Their requests were granted. Improvement
& prosperity attended them. This induced other con-
tiguous Tribes to request the same priviledge, &
others still adjoining them came forward with their
petitions. All were granted & the same regulations
established in every part. Within about three years
from the first establishment of the Empire, Lobaska
had the pleasure of seeing his son reign over a ter-

ritory of more than four hundred miles in length along the River Ohio, & of beholding a nation rapidly progressing from a state of barbarism, ignorance & wretchedness, to a state of civilization & prosperity.

Having now beheld the happy result of his experiment at Sciota, Lobaska made a second viset to Bambo king of Kentuck. The second son whose name was Hamback, was present at the city of Gamba at His youngest son Kalo attended him. He made known his plan of revolution to Bambo, who cordially acquiessed & called together his princes. They unanimously agreed to place Hamback on the throne of the Empire south of the Ohio River, & to ordain Kalo as their high Priest. With the exception of names & places the constitution of government was the same as that which the Sciotans adopted. The same measures were purpued to insure its success. A great & flourishing Empire arose & barbarous tribes connected themselves with the Empire, & under the fostering care of the government became wealthy civilized & prosperous.

Thus within the term of twelve years from the arival of Lobaska at Golanga, he had the satisfaction of beholding the great & benevolent objects which he had in view accomplished. He still continued his useful Labours & was the great Oricle of both Empires. His advice & sentiments were taken upon all important subjects, & no one ventured to controvert his opinions. He lived to behold the successful experiment of his institutions, & to see them acquire that strength & firmness as not easily to be overthrown.

Having acquired that renown & glory which are beyond the reach of envy, & which aspiring ambition would despair of attaining, at the age of eighty he bade an affectionate adieu to two Empires & left them to lament in tears his exile exit.

These two empires continued to progress in their improvements & population, & to rival each other in prosperity during the reign of Ten successive Emperors on the throne of Sciota. Peace & harmony & a friendly intercourse existed between them. No wars took place to disturb their tranquility, except what arose from the surrounding Savages, who sometimes disturbed the frontiers in a hostile manner for the sake of gaining plunder. But these attacks were generally repelled & defeated, without much loss of blood. They were in fact of such trifling consequence as to make no perceptible impediment to prevent the population improvement & prosperity of both Empires, & happy, thrice happy would it have been for them if they had still continued to have pursued the amicable & benevolent principles, which first marked the commencement & progress of their institutions.

## CHAT. X.

### MILETARY ARRANGEMENTS, AMUSEMENTS, CUSTOMS & EXTENT OF THE EMPIRES.

THE customs & amusements of a Nation evince the state of society which exists among the people. When the two Empires of Sciota & Kentuck had commenced their new career on the plan which was formed by Lobaska, they adopted as a true maxim that to avoid war it was necessary to be in constant preparation for it. It was the wise policy of of the two governments to make such military arrangements as never to be surprized by any enimy unprepared. In every city town & vilige the people were required to provide military impliments, & to deposit them in a secure place. These magazines were to contain a sufficient quantity of arms & warlike impliments to furnish every man who should be able to bear arms should be destitute. In order that every man might have sufficient skill to use them to advantage, great pains was taken to prepare him by teaching him the arts of war.

The knowledge of military tackticks as they it was then attainable, was likewise difused among the people. Young men from sixteen to twenty five years old were required to take the field four times in each year. & to spend sixteen days during each time in learning the military art, & in building fortifications. And very able-bodied men were required to spend eight days in each year in the same employments.

In consequence of these regulations a rivalship existed among the different sexions of the Empire to exceed each other in skill & dexterity in their military manoevers. Hence it was a general custom in every part of the country for different bodies of men to meet to engage in feigned battles once every year, in order to make a display of their improvements in the art of war. Premiums were given to those who were the most expert in shooting the arrow or in managing the spear & the sword.  Their amusements were generally of the athletick kind, calculated to improve their agility & strength & prepare them for warriors.  Wrestling, slinging, & throwing stones at marks, leaping ditches & fences & climbing trees & pricipices were some of their most favorite diversions. And as they took great pains to perfect themselves in these exercises, it would astonish Spectators of other nations, to observe the improvement they had made & the extraordinary feats of agility & strength which they exhibited.

Other diversions which had no tendency to fit them for war they seldom practiced, except when in the company of women, being taught by their religion the social virtues, they manifested a great regard for the rights of the other sex & always treated them with attention civility & tenderness.  Hence, when in the company of the fair sex it was curious to observe that when in the company of women they easily exchanged the warriors ruged & bold attitude of the bold warrior for the complasant & tender deportment of the affectionate galant.  The amusements which were pleasing to the female mind were equally pleasing to the men, whenever they held their social meeting for recreation.  These meetings were frequent among the younger class of Citizens, whether married or single.  Various kinds of amusements would frequently be introduced at such times for their mutual entertainment, but that which held the most conspicuous place was dancing.  But their manner of Dancing was different from that of the polished Europians.  Gracefulness & easy attitude were not so much studied in their movements as sprightliness & agility, & those tunes which admitted the greatest display of activity & sprightliness were generally the most pleasing fashionable. Hence those whose bodies were formed for the quickest movements if they keept time with the music, were the most admired. In small assemblies it was fashionable to amuse themselves with at playing with pieces of parchment. This they denominate the Bird Play. Each peice of is of an oval form & of convenient length & width & on each one is portraid the likeness of a Bird. All the birds of Prey that came within their knowledge have the honour of being represented on these peices of Parchment. On the other pieces are portraid other birds of different kinds The whole number of the peices amount to about sixty. These are promiscuous placed in a pack & dealt of to the company of players whose number does not exceed six. The person then, who has the greatest number of carnivorous Birds by a dextrous management, may catch the greatest number of the other Birds & thus obtain the victory.

During these enterviews of the different sexes & even in their common intercouse with each other they are always very cheerful & sociable & often display that fondness & familiarity, which in Europe would be considered as indicative of a lascivious character, but in this country are considered as what good manners requird. Nothing rude nothing indecent or immodest according to their ideas of the meaning of these terms, are admissible in company, & absolute lasciviousness would meet the most severe reprehension. When a young man wishes to settle himself in a family state he proclaims it by wearing a red feather in his cap. This is considered as an admonition to the young women who would not receive him for a husband, to avoid his company, whereas those whose inclinations towards him are more favourable admit his attentions. From this number he selects one as the object of his addresses. He obtains an enterview & proposes a courtship. If the proposition accords with her wishes, they then agree on a time when he shall make known the affair to her parents, whose approbation being obtained, he is then permited to viset her ten times in sixty days. At the expiration of this time the bargain for matrimony must be finished. Otherwise there must be a final termination of the courtshi or a postponement of the courtship, for the term of one year, or else a The parties are at liberty during the postponement to But if the parties are pleased with each other, the contract is made & the time for the celebra performance of the nuptial ceremonies is appointed. An entertainment is provided made friends are invited & the Bridegroom & the Bride present themselves in their best apparel. The company form a circle & they take their stand in the centre. The father of the Bride speaks. For what purpose do you present yourselves They answer, to join hands in wedlock. Our hearts are already joined, & we have made a solemn contract covenant to be true & faithful to each other. The company then all explain. "Blessings will attend

you if ye fulfil, but Curses if ye transgress. They
are then conducted into a log, round which a Rope is
tied. The Bride groom takes hold of one end of the
rope & the Bride the other, & being commanded to
draw the log into the house. They pull in opposite
directions with all their might. Having worried
themselves for some time to no purpose to the great
diversion of the company, the parents of both parties
step forward & giving them a severe reprimand, command them to draw in the same direction. They
instantly obey & the Log is easily drawn to its des-
tined place. The rest of the time is spent in great
cheerfulness, & meriment. They partake of the
entertainment & conclude with customary amusements. The Bridegroom & Bride are now desirous to
form a family by themselves. If their parents are of
sufficient ability they furnish them with a convenient
house & such furniture as will be required for family
use & such other property as they will need to enable
them to obtain a comfortable living. But if their
parents are poor they receive a pittance & contribu-
tions from relations & neighbours, & are placed in such
a situation that with proper industry & econimy they
can live live above indigence & enjoy life agreeably.
At the time they enter their new habitation they are
attended by Priests & by their relation & friends.
They kneel in the centre of the Room & the Priest
places his right hand on the head of the Bridegroom
& his left on the head of the Bride. After explaining
& enjoining in the most solemn manner the various
duties of the married state, he concludes his injunc-
tions with these words. "My Dear children, I con-

jure you as you regard your own peace & felicity, as
you would wish to acquire wealth & respectibility &
set an example worthy of emitation, that as you are
now yoked together to draw in the same direction.
They then rise & he presents each with a piece of
Parchment on which is written Draw in the same
direction All the duties of the conjugal state in
their opinion are comprized in this injunction Command.

As the Priests & the Censors were vigilent & careful to required to see that parents restrained the
vices of their children & instructed them in the
knowledge of their religious principles the effects
were very conspicuous.

Having been early taught to restrain the govern
their passions & to regard the practice of virtue as
their greatest good, it was generally the case that
love friendship & harmony existed in families. &
when parents were treated by their children with
great tenderness & respect

Parents manifested an anxious solicitude for the
future welfare & respectibility of their children, & in
their turn children treated their parents with respect
& reverence.  Nor did they forsake them in old age,
but paid provided liberally for their support &

But we are not to suppose that in the most virtuous age of the nation all were virtuous.  Far from
this.  But with such punctual exactness were the
laws executed, in the most prosperous state of the
nation, that vice & impiety had but few advocates &

the wicked were ashamed of their own characters. Tho' every vice was prohibited by law, yet the penalties were not severe. Murder alone was punished with death. With respect to other Laws, they were calculated to wound the pride & ambition of the transgressor, & produce shame & regret. Adultery was is punished by obliging the Culprit to wear a pair of Elk horns on his shoulders six days, & to walk thro' the City or vilage once each day, at which times the boys are at liberty to pelt him with rotten eggs. The thief is compelled to make ample restitution. For the third offense he is covered with tar & feathers & exhibited as a specticle for laughter & ridicule. Pugilists or boxers, if they are equally to blame for fighting, are yoked together at least one day, & in this situation are presented to the view of the multitude. They must wear the yoke until the quarrel is settled. Such being the nature of their penal laws & such the punctuality of executing the penalties on offenders that crimes were far less frequent in this country than in Europe, where the Laws are more severe, & offenders more often escape punishment. Tho' learning civilization & refinement had not arrived at that state of perfection, in which they exist in a great part of the Roman Empire, yet the two Empires of Sciota & Kentuck during their long period of peace & prosperity, were not less happy As luxury and extravagance were scarcely known to. exist especially among the common people, an happy equality was hence there was a great similarity in their manner of living, their dress, their habits & manners. Pride was not bloated & puffed

up with enormous wealth. Nor had envy fewel to
inflame her hatred & malice. As the two Empires
were not displeased with each others prosperity &
happiness & the two governments had no thirst nor
jealous of nor jealous of each others power, & as the
governments were not infested with a thirst for conquest, Peace of consequence waved her olive branch,
& the malignant passions lay dormant. Avarice &
corruption did not contaminate the ruling powers nor
bribery infest the seats of justice. The people felt
secure in the enjoyment of their rights, & desirous
to raise up families to partake of the same blessings
which they enjoyed

We can now trace the causes of their increase &
prosperity. To a religion which presented powerful
motives to restrain vice & impiety, & encourage virtue. To the difusion of a competent share of learning & knowledge to enable the people to understand
their right & enjoy the pleasures of social intercourse.
To the establishment of political institutions, which
gagrded property & life against oppressing injustice &
tyranny. To the knowledge which the people
obtained of agriculture & the mechanical arts & their
habits of industry & econimy. To the mild nature
of their laws & the certainty of executing the penalty
upon transgressors, & to such an equality of property
as to prevent the pride of wealth & the extravagance
of Luxury. To such causes may be ascribed the
rapid encrease of population, & the apparent contentment & felicity which extended thro' every part of
the country of the Empires. We might add like wise
the long peace that continued & the friendly inter-

course that existed between the two rival Empires.
A peace which had no interruption for the term of
near five hundred years. During this time their villages & cities were greatly enlarged, new settlements
were formed in every part of the country which had
not been inhabited, & towns a vast number of towns
were built, which rivaled as to number of inhabitants,
those which existed at the time their imperial governments were founded. Their settlements extended the
whole length of the great River Ohio to its confluence
with the Mississippi, & over the whole country on
both sides of the Ohio River, which are watered by
streams which empty into it. And also along the
great lakes of Eri & Mishigan, & even some settlements were formed in some parts of the country
which borders on Lake Ontario. Such was the vast
extent of the country which they inhabited, & such
the fertility of the soil, that many milions were easily
fed & supported with such a plenty, & competence of
provision as was necessary for their comfort & happiness.

During the time of their rising greatness & tran-
quillity, their policy led them to fortify the country in
every part, the interior as well as the frontiers. This
they did partly for their own safety, provided a war
should take place, & they should be invaded by an
enimy, & partly to keep alive a military & improve a
warlike spirit, & the knowledge of military tackticks.
Near every vilage or City they constructed forts or
fortifications These were generally of an oval form &
of different dimentions according to the number of
inhabitants who lived in the town. The Ramparts or

walls were formed of dirt which was taken in front of the fort. A deep canal or trench would likewise be formed. This would still increase the dificulty of surmounting the walls in front In addition to this they inserted <u>sticks</u> pieces of Timber on the top of the Ramparts. These peices were about seven feet in length from the ground to top, which was sharpned. The distance between each piece was about six inches, thro' which they would shoot their arrows against an Enimy. Some of their fortifications have two Ramparts which run paralel with each other, built in the same manner with a distance between of about two or three perches. Their gates are strong & well constructed for defense. Within these forts are likewise a number of small houses, for the accommodation of the army & inhabitants, in case of an invasion & likewise a storehouse for the reception of provisions & arms. A country thus fortified, containing so many milions of inhabitants hearty & robust & with habits formed for war, might well be supposed as able to defend themselvs against an invading enimy. If they were beat from the frontier, they would still retreat back to the fortifications in the interior & there make a successful stand. But what avails all the wisdom, the art & the works of men, what avails their valour their strength & numbers, when the Almighty God is provoked to chastise them, & to execute his vengeance in their overthrow & destruction.

# CHAT. XI.

As the Sciotans & the Kentucks had maintained with each other an unterrupted peace & friendly intercourse for the space of four hundred & eighty years, it seems almost incredible that a Cause which was of no great importance to either nation, should excite their resentment against each other & produce all the horrors of war. But such was the unhappy effect of an affair, which had no regard to a single person except the imperial families of the two empires & the king of Sciota. As the families had were dessended from the great Lobaska, they had during the reign of all their Emperors been in the habit of visiting each other, but as each Emperor & his children were required not to marry out of their respective dominions, no intermariages had taken place. They however claimed relationship, & still continued to each other the appelation of our dearest & best beloved Cousen.

A Cousen of this description, who was the eldest son of Hamboon, the Emperor of Kentuck arrived at the City of Golanga with a small but splendid retinue of Friends. At that time Rambock, who was the fourteenth Emperor, was seting on the throne of Sciota. He received the young Prince with apparent sensation of the highest pleasure, & spared no pains to manifest towards him by his treatment the greatest esteem & friendship. The Emperor had an only son

whose name was Moonrod. He ordered him to attend
the young prince & to treat him with every token of
affection & honour. They spent their time in receiving visets from the officers of the government, in
viewing curiosities, & in the assemblies of the first
Class of young citizens who met for recreation.

Elseon, for this was the name of the young prince,
was soon after his arival introduced to Lamesa, the
eldest daughter of the Emperor. She was a young
Lady of a very fair & beautiful countenance. Her
features & the construction of her person were formed
to please the fancy, whilst the ease & gracefulness &
modesty of her deportment, were very pleasing to all
her acquaintance. Her mind was replenished with
the principles of knowledge & virtue & such was her
vivacity and the ease with which she expressed her
ideas, that all were delighted with her conversation.
No wonder that this fair imperial dansel attracted the
attention of Elsion, & at their first enterview enkindled
a spark in his boosom, which he could hardly prevent
from being discovered thro his blushing countanance, & the embarassment he felt in conversation.
He strove to erase those tender impressions which
she had made on his heart, but in vain; every
renewed enterview only served only to fix her image
deeper in his mind with & to make the flame of Love
more difficult to extinguish. He reasoned on the
obsticles in the way of obtaining this young lady for
his partner, but instead of cooling only ser it only
increased the ardor of his passion, & produced a
resolution that with the consent of Lamesa, nothing
should prevent the attainment of his wishes.

To a mind thus ardent which possessed the native courage, resolution & perseverance of Elseo, the most gigantic obsticles would vanish into vapour. Nor was it long before he found that a correspondent passion was excited in her breast. The moment she first saw him, her heart palpitated, her face was covered with crimson, she turned her eyes & attempted to speak, her tongue stopt its motion in the midle of a period. She hamed, sat down & observed that she was not well. A description of this scene is painted by a Sciotan bard in poetic numbers. He represents the young Lady as recovering in a short time from this state of agitation & confusion, & as being afterwards composed & having a better command of her passions. To follow the poet in the description which he gives of Elseon, to whom he attaches a countenance & figure superior to other mortals, & qualities which produced the universal esteem & admiration. would not comport with the faithful page of history. Suffice it to say that Lamesa was captivated with his person, & was impressed with those ideas & sentiments that her happiness fled except when she either enjoyed or anticipated his company. After Elsion had firmly determined to marry Lamesa, he was impatient for a private enterview with her to disclose his sentiments. This occured in a short time. They were together in one of the apartments of the Emperors palace, the company had all retired. I have, said he in a low voice to Lamesa, conceived that opinion of you that I hope you will not be displeased if I express my feelings with frankness & sincerity. You must, she replied, be the best judge of what it is proper for you to express. I am always pleased with sincerity. As the sun, says he, my dear Lamesa, when he rises with his radiant beams, dispels the darkness of knight, so it is in your power to dispel the clouds of anxiety that rest upon my soul. The Crown of Kentuck will be like a Rock on my head, unless you will condesend to share with me the glory & felicity of my reign. Will you consent to be my dearest friend & companion for life? There is nothing, she replies, would give me more pleasure than a compliance with your request, provided it shall meet the approbation of my Father. But how can he consent, when our Constitution requires that his daughters should marry in his own domin- ions? Beside, my father intends that I shall receive the King of Sciota for my husband. By perform- ming, says he, the cerimonies of maraige at Talanga, we shall literally comply with the imperial constitu- tion, as Talanga is within the dominions of your Father. But as for the King of Sciota, do you sin- cerely wish to have him for a husband? No, she quickly replies, speaks anger sparkled in her eyes. No. the King of Sciota for my husband. His pride, his haughtiness, the pomposity of all his movements excite my perfect disgust. I should as leave be yoked to a porcupine. Several

These Lovers, as you may well conjecture, said many things too tender & endearing to please the taste of the common Class of Lovers. In this enter- view which lasted about four hours, they exchanged the most transporting expression of love, made the most solemn protests vows of sincerity & perpetual friendship & finally agreed that Elseon should make known to the Emperor their mutual desire to be joined in wedlock. The next day he wrote to the Emperor as follows.

May it please your most excellent Majesty. Permit me to express my most sincere gratitude for the high favors & honour, which thro' the beneficence of of your Majesty I have enjoyed in your dominions. I am likewise impelled to request a favour, which to me would be the most precious gift, that is in the power of your Majesty to bestow. Having contracted an acquaintance with your most amiable daughter Lamesa, & finding that a correspondent affection & esteem exist in our hearts toward each other & a mutual desire to be united by the solemn covenant of maraige, I would therefore solicit your Majesty's permission that such a connection be formed.

Such a connection I conceive, may in its effect be very salutary & beneficial to bothe Empires. It will unite the two imperial families in a nearer in the bond of consanguinity, & fix upon them an additional obligation to cultivate friendship, peace & an amiable intercourse. It will strengthen the sinues of both governments & promote & promote an happy interchange of friendly offices. As to the objection that might arise from the constitution requiring, that the Emperors daughters should marry in his own dominions, this according to its literal meaning can have respect only to the place where the Emperors daughter shall marry. If by your Majestys permission, I should marry your daughter Lamesa in your dominions it will be a literal fulfillment of the consti-

tution. From this ground therefore, I conceive that
no objection of any weight can arise. Will your
majesty please to vouchsafe me an answer to my
request.

Signed. ELSEON. PRINCE OF KENTUCK.

This letter was presented to the Emperor by
Helicon, an intimate friend of Elseon. The Emperor
read it assumed the aspect of deep consideration,
walked the room a few moments, then took a seat
& told Helicon that he might inform the young
prince that he should receive an answer in a ten
days.

But why this few Ten days, a long time for two
ardent lovers to remain in suspense. But the Emperor must consult his counsellors, his priests & the
last & most fatal counsellor of all the King of Sciota,
who presumed to claim the hand of the fair Lamesa.
The affair became public. The popular sintiment at
first favoured the connection. The Emperors counsellors & his priests were at first inclined to recom-
mend an affirmative answer. But the interest of the
Sciotan King soon prevailed. This produced a different view of the subject The Counsellors perceived
that such a connection would be a most flagrant
violation of the true meaning & spirit of the constitution, & the priests considered that it would be an act
of the greatest impiety, as it transgress an explicit
injunction of the great founder of their government
& religion. This opinion had vast Weight on the
minds of a great majority of the people. The more
liberal sort vindicated the cause of Elseon. This

produced a great debate altercation & confusion thro'
the City. All were anxious to know the Emperors
decision.

On the tenth day the Emperor transmitted to the
prince the following answer to his letter.

To our best beloved Cousen Elseon Prince of Kentuck. The letter we received from your highness has
impressed our hearts with a deep sense of the honor
& benefit, which you intended uor family & Empire.
At first we were inclined to accept of the alliance you
proposed. But having examined & considered the
subject with great seriousness & attention, we that
find that to admit your Highness who is not a citizen
of our Empire to marry into our family, would be a
most flagrant violation of the true meaning & spirit
of our constitution. & an impious outrage on the
sacred memory of its Founder For these reasons we
must solicit your Highness not to insist on our compliance with your request.

Signed.    HAMBOCK, EMPEROR OF SCIOTA.

As Elseon had been informed of the complexion
which his affairs had assumed in the court, & thro'
the City, he was prepared for the alswer which he
received.

Without manifesting the least chagrin or Resentment, he appeared to acquiesse in the decision of the
Emperor. He displayed his in his countenance, his
conversation & deportment, his usual cheerfulness
& vivacity. He continued his amusements & associated with company with the same ease, gracefulness
& dignified conduct which he had done before. At

the same time, his determination was fixed to transport the fair Lamesa into his fathers dominions. The
first enterview he had with her after he received the
Emperors letter, he informed her of its contents. She
trembled, paleness began to cover her face, & had
not Elseon received her into his arms, perhaps she
would have falen from her seat However, by a few
soothing words and caresses, she was restored to her
former composure & recollection. Believe me, quoth
he, my Dearest Lamesa, you shall be mine. This
heart shall be torn from my bosom, & these limbs
from my body, nothing else shall prevent our union
& compleat enjoyment of happiness. Can the ancient
scribbling of a great sage or the degree of an Emperor prevent the streams from uniting with the ocean?
With the same ease & propriety can they prevent the
union of our hands, since our hearts are united.
With your consent, you shall be mine. ˙ Is it possible,
she replies, is it possible to disregard the authority
of an indulgent & beloved parent & disobey his command. This I never did. What if he should command you, says Elseao, to marry the King of Sciota?
would you obey? He might, she replies, with more
regard to my happiness, command me to plunge a
dagger into my heart. I cannot endure that super-
cilious bundle of pride & affectation.

At this moment her maid entered the room &
gave her a letter. I received this letter, she says,
from your Brother, who told me it was from the
Emperor. She opened it & read.

*My Dearest & best beloved Daughter.*

Having the most tender & affectionate

regard for your future welfare & felicity, we have
concluded a treaty of marriage between you &
Lambul the King of Sciota. This alliance will be
honourable to our family & be productive of many
benefits to the Empire. On the tenth day from this
time the nuptial ceremonies will be celebrated, con-
summated in our Palace. You will be in readiness &
yield a cheerful compliance with our will.

Signed. BAMBOCK. EM'R OF SCIOTA.

Had the lightning flashed from the clouds & pierced
her heart, it could not have produced a more instantaneous effect. She fell into the arms of Elseon, the
maid ran for a cordial. Elseon rubed her temples
& hands & loosened the girdle about her waist.
Within about an hour her blood began to circulate.
Elseon to his inexpressible joy felt her pulse begin
to beat, & perceived flashes of colour in her face.
With a plaintive groon, she once more opened her
eyes to the beams of day, & in a kind of wild dis-
traction exclaimed, Ah cruel, cruel Father, why have
you doomed your daughter to a situation the most
odious & disgustful. As well might you have thrown
her into a den of porcupines, opossums & serpents.
With such animals I could enjoy life with less disgust
& torment, than with this mighty King of Sciota, and
An alliance with him an honour to our family, an
honour to the descendants of the great Lobaska!
What wicked counsellors have deceived my Father, &
induced him to throw me into the arms of this hateful
monster? Ah, whither shall I fly & escape my bar-
berous destiny. I am your protector, says Elseon. I
am your friend & will conduct you beyond the loving

& gigantic grasp of Sambol. His loathsome arms shall never encircle my dear Lamesa. Consent to my request & we will be within ten days at the City of Gamba. There you will be esteemed as the brightest Orniment of my Fathers Empire. No longer Oh Elseon, she exclaimed, can I refuse my consent to your proposal. When a compliance with my fathers commands will entail wretchedness & misery thro' life. Heaven will pardon my disobedience. Yes, Elseo, I will go with you, & place my happiness in your power. rather than fall into the hands of this haughty Sambul.

What could she say more to excite the feelings of a heart struggling under the operation of different passions & opposite motives. She has taken her resolution, love has gained the preeminence over every obsticle

At this resolution, Elseon was transported with joy. He now proceeded to form his plans for their flight. On the fourth day after, he called upon the Emperor & requested his permission to depart to his own Country. The Emperor importuned him to tarry & be one of the guests at Lamesas wedding. But he declined by urging as his apology the anxiety & impatience of his father for his return. Permission was granted, & the Emperor aded that he should do himself the honour to furnish the prince with an escort when he left the city. Elseon replied that as he was not fond of much parade, he would wish that the escort might not consist of the Emperors soldiers,

only his friend & his daughter & with with each of
them a friend. These says he, are my dearest & best
beloved cousens, for whom I shall ever retain the
most sincere friendship. Nothing can afford me
more pleasure, says the Emperor, than to comply
with your request.

Elseon took an affectionate leave of the Emperor
& on the second day after, being prepared for his
journey he set off with his three friends & their servants. Moonrod, prince of the Empire, & Lamesa
with her two sisters, with each of them a friend,
attended them on his journey about twenty miles.
They all tarried at a vilage over night.

Imagination alone can paint the pleasant & happy
scene. Elseon was transported with joy. He prest
her to his bosom with all the ardor of inthusiasm, &
she yielded to all his tender & innocent embraces
with a grateful sensibility & modest resignition.

The invention & ingenuity of Elseon must now
be employed in forming a plan for their flight to his
Fathers dominions. As he appeared to acquiesse in
the decision of the Emperor, & had maintained the
same cheerful deportment, none were suspicious of
his design. The Emperor & the whole court still
manifested toward him every token of high respect &
sincere friendship. Without any hesitation, the
Emperor complied with his request that his dear
cousins, the son & the three daughters of the
Emperor, with each of them a friend, should accom-
pany him about twenty miles on his return to Kentuck. The retinue of the young Prince consisted of

four of his most intimate friends & their servants.
He took care to send their baggage on by two servants one day before they set out. The morning
arived, the sun shone with radiant splendor, not a
cloud intervened or was seen to float in the atmosphere. It was the fourth day after Lamesa had
received the letters which doomed her to the embraces
of Sambul. The Emperor, his Counsellors, his Priests
& principal officers assembled, & having invited the
young prince & his friends to meet them, they
entered the circle with great ceremony. The Emperor then addressed the Young Prince, thanked
him for the honour of his viset & expressed his firm
determination, to maintain a sincere friendship & an
inviolable peace with the government of Kentuck.
Elseon replied that the whole sentiments would meet
the cordial approbation of his Father, who retained
the same sentiments of friendship & peace toward
the government of Sciota. He then thanked the
Emperor & the whole assembly for the high respect
they had shown him. This was done with that frankness & apparent sincerity that the whole assembly
were highly pleased. The Emperor then embraced
him & gave him his blessing. Customary ceremonies
were mutually exchanged by the whole company, &
even tears were seen to drop from every eye.

    As the whole of this parade indicates no flight of
Elseon & Lamesa, we must now view them with their
select company of friends setting out on a short
journey. All mounted on horses, they rode about
twenty miles to a village where they halted. An eligant supper was provided, they were chearful &

sociable, none appeared more so, that Elseon &
Lamesa. The next day Elsean requested the company of his dear cousens a short distance on his
journey. When they had rode about two miles they
halted & proposed to take their leave of each other
Lamesa & her friend, without being perceived by the
company rode on. It was a place where the road
turned, & by riding one rod, they could not be seen.
The rest of the company entered into a short conversation & passed invitation for reciprocal visets &
friendly offices. They then clasped each others
hands & bowing very low, took an affectionate fare-
well. But where are Lamesa & her friend? During
these ceremonies their horses move with uncommon
swiftness, her heart palpitates with an apprehension
that she might be overtaken by her brother. But
now a friend more dear, her beloved Elseon, with his
companions, outstrip the wind in their speed. &
within one hour & half they overtake these fearful
Damsels. They all precipitate their course, casting
their eyes back every moment to no purpose. her
pursuers. But pursuers had not sufficient time to
overtake them. They safely arive on the Bank of
the Great River. Elseon & Lamesa were the first
that entered the boat, the rest follow. & such was
Elseons engagedness & anxiety to secure his fair
prize, that he even seized an oar and used it with
great strength & dexterity. As their feet stept on the
opposite shore, Elseon claspt his hands & spoke
aloud, Lamesa is mine. She is now beyond the grasp
of a pompous tyrant, & the control of a father whose
mind is blinded by the sordid advice of a menial

junto of counsellors & priests. She is mine & shall
soon be the Princess of Kentuck. Their movement is
no slow thro' the remaining part of their journey.
They at length arive at the great City of Gamba.
We may now contemplate them as having new scenes
to pass thro' Not to delineate the parade which was
made at the court of Hamboon, for the reception of
his son, Lamesa, & their friends, or to describe the
joy that was exhibited in every part of the city on
their arival, & the universal surprize occasioned by
the story of the flight of these two Lovers. Suffice it
to say, that those who beheld Lamesa did not blame
Elseon.

As Hamboon was not very punctilious in his regard
for the constitution, being possessed of very liberal
sentiments, Elseon found no difficulty in obtaining
his consent to marry Lamesa. On the fourth day
after their arival, Elseon & Lamesa, with each of
them a friend appeared on a stage, which was erected
on the public square of the City. The Emperor &
Empress with his counsellors, his Priests his officers,
& all his relations, with the principal Ladies of the
City, formed a procession & surrounded the stage.
The common Citizens being a great multitude, took
their stands as they pleased. The Emperor &
Empress then mounted the stage, & united Elseon &
Lamesa in the bond of wedlock according to custom.
& as pulling the Log was an indespensible ceremony
one was provided with a rope around it on the stage.
The Bridegroom & Bride played their parts in pulling
the rope with such dexterity & gracefulness, that the
whole assembly was most pleasingly entertained.

When all was ended, the whole assembly claped their hands & cried, Long live Elseon & Lamesa. & giving three huzzas, the common citizens dispersed. The rest repaired to a sumptuous entertainment, & spent the remaining part of the day & evening in conversation, singing & recreation.

## CHAP XII.

THE reader will recollect that Elseon & his friends left Moonrod & his friends in a very pleasant mood without the least suspicion, that Lamesa & her friend had deserted them. When they had arrived at the vilage, what was their surprize when they found that Lamesa & her friend were not in the company, nor had any one any recollection of her being in company, after they had stopped to take their leave of Elseon. Moonrod & the other gentlemen immediately rode back with the greatest speed to the place where they had halted, & not finding any traces of her Lamesa the conclusion was then certain that she had prefered the company of the young Prince & was on her way to Kentuck.

Pursuit would be in vain. Their only alternative was to hasten back to carry the doleful intelligence to the Emperor. Their speed was nearly equal to that of Elseon. Without waiting to perform the customary ceremony of entering the palace, Moonrod immediately rushed into the Emperors presence, & exclaimed, your daughter Lamesa has been seduced by Elseon to leave our company unperceived, & has gone with him to Kentuck. Nothing but the pencil

of the Limner, could paint the Astonishment of the
Emperor. He rose, stood motionless for a moment,
then staring fiercely on Moonrod he spoke. is it possible, is it possible, are you not mistaken my Son. I
am not, says he, my most excellent Father. I am
not mistaken. This morning we attended Elseon a
small distance from the village where we lodged.
When we had halted to take our leave & our attention
was all engaged she & her friend she & her friend
rode off unperceived by any of our company nor did
we miss her until we arived again at the vilage. We
have made full search & enquiry, & find that she has
absolutely gone with the young prince to Kentuck.
What an ingrate says the Emperor, what a monster
of hipocrisy Did the honourable attention we have
shown him demand such treatment? How has he
insulted the dignity of our family & outraged the
high authority of our government. This affair will
demand the most serious consideration. O Lamesa,
Lamesa, my darling my best beloved child, was it
possible for you to be so deceived by that artful
prince, was it possible for you to disobey the command of your indulgent father? as they stept on the
covering top of the canal, the thin pieces of timber
broke & they all plunged in & found themselves in an
instant at the bottom of the canal. Surprised & terrified & they soon found themselves in no situation to
vindicate their exclusive right to wear blue feathers
in their caps. They were compleatly in the power of
their enimies who returned quick upon them They
demanded quarter & surrendered themselves pris-

oners of war. And giving up their arms, their demand was granted. In the meantime a party of Sciotans who lay in ambush, on the side of the Hill rushed down upon the reserved corps of the Kentucks, who being filled with consternation at the direful disaster of their companions, surrendered themselvs prisoners of war without a struggle. Thus in a few moments, by pursuing the stratigem or plan of Lobaska, An army of thirty Thousand men were captured, & the pride & haughtiness of a mighty Prince was humbled. Not a drop of blood was shed to accomplish the whole.

& bring upon our family such wretchedness & dishonour. Fame with Her Thousand tongues commenced her pleasing employment, & as swift as the wings of Time she wafted the inteligence thro' the City with many distorted & exaggerated particulars. All was astonishment confusion & uproar. Resentment enkindled her indignant sparks into a flame & the general cry was revenge & war. The Sciotan King was walking in his parlour, feeding his imagination with the pleasing prospect of his future glory & felicity. I am, quoth he to himself, honoured above all the other princes of the Empire, & even above the heair apparent to the imperial crown of Kentuck. Who could be admitted except myself to marry this fair Lamesa, the eldest daughter of the Emperor, the most amiable the most accomplished & the most honorable Lady in the universe. This is a distinction which will place me on equal ground with the

Emperor himself, & command from all my subjects
the homage of their highest respect and reverence.
Besides I have a soul that can relish the charms of
the beautiful maid. She will adore me as her Lord &
think herself highly honoured & exceeding happy to
submit to my most endearing & affectionate
embraces. But ah, mighty Sambul, you little
tho't how soon this delightful prospect would be
reversed, & that your soul would be filled with
chagrin indignation & revenge. A messenger burst
into his parlour & announced the astonishing tidings
of Lamesas elopement. She had absolutely gone,
says he, to become the wife of Elseon, & the empress
of Kentuck. Not the wondrous & instantaneous
roar of ten Thousand thunders instantaneously
thro' the atmosphere, could have produced greater
surprise. His countanance was all amazement It was
for a moment covered with paleness, his lips quiv-
ered, his knees smote together & his gigantic body
trembled like the shaking of a tower under the effects
of an earthquake. But soon after a little silent his
reflections & cogitations caused the blood to return
with a ten-fold velocity into his face. it assumed the
colour of redness & clinching He assumed the attitude of terrific majesty & poured forth his feelings in
a voice more terrible than the roaring of a volcano.
How have I been abused, dishonoured, insulted &
outraged. How have my prospects of glory been
instantaneously blasted & my character, my character
become the ridicule of a laughing world. What
felicities of enjoying the imperial maid in my arms,

adoring me for her husband are now vanished. & by whom am I thus disgraced insulted & injured? By the mock prince of Kentuck, an effeminate stripling, a cringing & plausible Upstart. He has robed me of the fairest orniment of my kingdom, she Lamesa, who was mine by solemn contract, & must he now revel in her charms which are mine, & pride himself in those deceitful arts by which he has seduced her, & stolen her from my enjoyment? No, ungrateful & insidious monster, your triumph shall be of short duration, & this arm shall viset your crimes upon your head with a ten-fold vengence. Having poured forth a torrent of the most dreadful imprecations & menaces, he left his parlour & walked forth to consult his principal officers on the best plan to obtain revenge.

In the meantime the Emperor, less haughty & indignant, & possessed of sentiments more humane & benelent, sent an invitation to his Counsellors to attend him. They were unanimous in the opinion that the offense of Elseon required reparation. But should war be the consequence, if he refused to return Lamesa? On this question, two of the counsellors contended that an humble recantation would repair the injury done to the honour of the imperial family, & the authority of the government. The other two insisted that they should demand in addition that would not be sufficient But that they should demand in addition ten Mammouth which would be an adequate compensation, but they all depreciated the horrors of war. In the midst of their debetes which were managed with great coolness & imparti-

ality, Sambul presented himself. I have come forward
says he, may it please your most excellent majesty,
to demand the fulfillment of that solemn contract,
which you made to deliver me your eldest daughter
in marriage.    She has been surreptitiously carried
off by the young prince of Kentuck.    She is mine by
contract & your majesty is bound to deliver her to me.
I demand Let her be immediately demanded, & if the
Emperor the father of the young prince shall refuse
to return her, this will implicate him in the same crime
& be a sufficient cause of war.    In that case war will
be indespensible to vindicate the honour of our
respective crowns, & the rights of the Empire.    I
should then give my voice for war, & would then
never sheathe my sword until the torrents of blood
had made expiation for the ingratitude baseness &
perfidy of the young Princy.    An humble recantation or the delivery of ten mammouth, would this be
a sufficient reparation for such an offense so flagitious?    No, the very proposal would be an insult on
the dignity of our government.    Can anything short
of the repossession of the fair object stolen, of the
invaluable prize felonously taken from us, be an
adequate compensation?    Nothing short of this can
heal our bleeding honour.  appease the indignation
of our subjects, & reinstate friendship & and an amicable intercouse, between both Empires.    Let this be
your demand that Lamesa shall be returned.    Let a
refusal be followed by an immediate declaration of
war, Let the resources & energies of the nation be
called forth.    Assemble your armies & pour destruction upon all who shall oppose the execution of our

revenge. I myself will lead the van & mingle my arm
with those who fight the most bloody battles. Heroes
shall fall before us, their towns shall be laid in ruins,
& carnage shall glut our indignant Swords.

When further deliberation had taken place, the
Emperor & two of his counsellors adopted the advice
of Sambul to demand Lamesa & an envoy was
immediately dispatched to the Emperor of Kentuck
with the following Letter.

May it please your most gracious majesty. Nothing could have given us more pleasure than the disposition you manifested in sending Elseon, the heir
apparent to your crown to viset our family. We
treated him as our dearest Cousen & as our most
intimate friend. He was invited to associate with our
children, & to consider himself whilst he tarried as a
member of our family. Such being the confidence
we placed in his rectitude & honour, that he assumed
the liberty to contract the most intimate acquaintance with Lamesa, our eldest daughter. This produced an agreement between them, that with our
consent they would be united in marriage. Nothing
could have been more pleasing than such a connection. But we found that it would be a most flagrant
violation of the true meaning & spirit of our constitution, & an impious outrage on the memory of its
great founder. For these reasons, we signified our
pleasure that Elseon would not insist on our compliance with his request. He appeared to acquiesse
in our decision. & we afterwards contracted with
Sambul, King of Sciota to give her in marriage to
him.

But the after conduct of your son, may it please your most gracious majesty, did not correspond with the high confidence we placed in him. With deep regret & the most painful sensations we are compeled to declare that he has committed a crime which has disturbed our peace & happiness, dishonoured our family & outraged the authority of our government, & the rights of our Empire. He has formed a plan to transport Lamesa into your dominions. To accomplish this, he made use of the most insidious arts, He took advantage of our clemency & indescretion, & the high respect we manifested toward him, & without our consent & contrary to our will, he has succeeded in transporting to the City of Gamba. in his perfidious design. Lamesa is doubtless with you in the City of Gamba. A crime which of such malignity, committed against the honour & interest & dignity of our family government & Empire demands reparation. Your majesty will perceive that the only adequate reparation which can be made, will be the return of Lamesa to our dominions. We therefore demand that she be conveyed back with all possible expidition.

No other alternative can prevent the interruption of that confidence friendship & peace, which have long continued between both Empires, & save them from the horrors & calamities of war.

Signed. RAMBOCK, EMPEROR OF SCIOTA.

When Hamboon had received this letter, he immediately invited his counsellors to attend him, & laid it before them, & as it was a subject of vast impor-

tance to the Empire, he likewise invited his priests &
principal officers to join them in council. The various passions appeared to operate in the course of
their consultation. To avoid Hostilities, with all its
attendant calamities, was what they most ardently
desired, & some contended that if no other alternative could be agreed upon, it would be for the interest of the Empire & the best policy to return the
princess. but others reprobated this measure as
pusilanimous, & cowardly & advised if no other reparation would be received, to retain the princess &
maintain the conflict with a manly & heroic firmness.
What, say they, do not honour & justice require that
we should defend the rights of the imperial family?
If the Sciotan government should demand that we
should send them our Emperor or Empress, would
not honour impel us to spurn at the demand, & reject
it with indignation? Their present demand is as pre-
posterous & as insulting. No satisfaction will they
receive for the supposed injury, except that we
should seize the Princess of the Empire, tare her
from the bosom of her consort & transport her to
Sciota. Are we capable of an act so unjust & inhu-
man, so base & disgraceful? As the debate was proceeding Elseon rose. May I says he—claim your
attention a moment. Undaunted by the cruel
demand & haughty menace of the Sciotan government, I am willing to abide your decision. If transporting Lamesa into our dominions when she had
been most unjustly & inhumanly denied me for a
companion, is a crime so perfidious & flagitious as of
such magnitude, then inflict a punishment that shall

be adequate to the offense. But if the Almighty, whose benevolence is infinite, has designed the union of hands where hearts are united, I have then transgressed no divine law, but have obeyed the divine will. I am therefore innocent of any crime. I have an undoubted right to retain Lamesa for my wife, & no government on earth have any authority from heaven to tear her from my bosom. Nor will I submit to such an event, so long as the life blood circulates thro' my heart & warms my limbs. If war must be the consequence of my proceedings, which transgressed no principle of honour justice or humanity, were both innocent & honourable, it will give me the most painful feelings. I shall deplore its calamities, but will never shrink like a Dastard from the conflict. The Sciotan King, who is at the bottom of all the mischief shall never behold me fleeing before his gigantic sword, or skulking to avoid a single combat with him. You have therefore no other alternative but either first to slay your prince, & then like cowards to send back your princess to Sciota, or else to make immediate preparations to meet their threatened vengeance, with fortitude & courage.

This speach of the young prince united the whole council. & they unanimously agreed to reject the demand of the Sciotan government. A letter was written & an Envoy dispatched, with instructions to attempt a reconciliation. He precipitated his journey to the court of Rambock, & when he arrived, he delivered him the following letter.

May it please your most excellent Majesty. Next

to the welfare & prosperity of our Empire, we should rejoice in the welfare & prosperity of yours. It is therefore with extreme regret that we view the unhappy difference, which has arisen & which threatens to involve the two Empires in the calamities of war.

Had you demanded a reparation for the supposed injury which which would consist with the principles of justice & the honour of our crown & government, it should be given you with the utmost cheerfulness. But to return you Lamesa, who has now become the princess of Kentuck, would be tearing her from the arms of an affectionate husband & breaking the bond of solemn wedlock. As the compliance with your demand, will subject us to the commission of such an injustice & cruelty, it must therefore be our duty to declare that we will not return the young princess. & as such an event would destroy her happiness as well as that of her affectionate consort, we shall permit her to tarry in our dominions & grant her protection. We are however desirous that an honourable reconciliation may take place, & a good understanding be restored. To effect this most important & very desirable object, we have given full authority to Labanko our beloved brother, the bearer of this Letter, to negotiate a settlement of our difference. provided you will receive anything as a substitute for what the object you have demanded.

Signed. HAMBOON, EMPEROR OF KENTUCK.

The mind of Rambock was not formed for the perpetual exercise of resentment, & malice, & having conversed a considerable time with Labanco, who apologized for the conduct of the young prince with great ingenuity his anger abated & he felt a disposition for the negotiation of friendship. But the indignation & malice of Sambul encreased with time, his dark soul thirsted more ardently for revenge, & nothing would satisfy but blood & carnage. He employed instruments to assist in faning the spark of resentment, & blowing them into the flames of war. Not content to represent facts as they existed, & in their true colours, monstrous stories were fabricated & put in circulation, calculated to excite prejudice & rouse the resentment of the people against Elseon, & the whole Empire of Kentuck. He had recourse to a class of men who were denominated prophets & conjurors to favour his designs. They had for many ages a commanding influence on the minds of a great majority of the people. As they pretended to understand, have art of investigating the councils & designs of the heavenly Hierarchy, & to have a knowledge of future events, the people listened with pleasure to their representations. predictions & tho't it impious to question or doubt their fulfilment A small company of these necromanceers or juglers assembled on the great square of the City, & mounted a stage which was provided for them. The citizens attended It was a prodigious concourse of all classes of citizens The of all descriptions both wise & simple, both male & female. They surrounded the stage & were all attention. All anxious to learn the decrees of heaven, & the future destinies of the Empire. Drofalick, their chief prophet extended his arms & cast up his eyes to-Heaven. Quoth he, Heaven

unfolds her massy gates, & opens to my view a prospect wide & vast. The seven sons of the great Spirit
seize their glittering swords, & swear that they shall
not be sheathed till blood in torrents run & deluge
the fair land of Kentuck I behold armies martialing
on the celestial plain, & hear warriors & heroes cry,
Avenge the crime of Elseon. I hear a thundering.
voice proceeding from the great throne of him who
rules the world, proclaiming thus, Corn shall not
grow in the Sciotan fields nor mammouth yield their
milk, nor fish be taken in the snare but pestilence
shall roam, unless Sciota shall avenge the crime of
Elseon. Drofalick ended his prophesy. Hamack
then arose & in his hand he held a stone which he
pronounced transparent. Thro' this he could view
things present & things to come. could behold the
dark intriques & cabals of foreign courts, & behold
discover hidden treasures, secluded from the eyes of
other mortals. He could behold the galant & his
mistress in their bedchamber, & count all their moles
warts & pimples. Such was the clearness of his
sight, when this transparent stone was placed before
his eyes. He looked firmly & steadfastly on the
stone & raised his prophetick voice. I behold Hamboon with all his priests & great officers assembled
around him With what contempt he declares he
despises all the Sciotans. They are, says he, cowards & poltroons. They dare not face my brave
warriors. Here I see four men coming forward bear-
ing an image, formed with all the fetures of ugliness
& deformity. This they called Sambul the King of
Sciota, the whole company break forth into boister-

ous Laughing. Ah, see & they are cuting off his
head with their swords. Yes, & are now kicking it
about the palace. Here is a pole. it is stuck upon
that & carried thro' the City. Oh my loving sparks,
Elseon & Lamesa, what makes you so merry? Why
Elseon says he has outwitted the Sciotans, he has
got the prize & he little regards their resentment.
Hamack was proceeding with such nonsensical visions, when the whole multitude interrupted him with
a cry, Revenge, Revenge, We will convince the
Kentuckans that we are not cowards or poltroons.
Their heads shall pay for their sport in kicking
about the pretended head the head of our pretended
beloved King We will avenge the crime of Elseon.
The great & good Being is on our side & threatens us
with famine & pestilence, unless we avenge the crime
of Elseon.

The arts of the Conjurers were the consummation
of Sambuls plan to produce in the minds of the multitude an enthusiasm & rage for war. He now repairs
to the Emperor & solicits him to assemble his counsellors immediately, proclaim war & concert measures
for its prosecution. The Emperor replies that they
should soon be assembled, but as to war, it was a
subject which reguired great consideration.

Early on the next day his counsellors-priests &
principal officers met him in the council room. He
laid before them the Letter of Hamboon, & added
observed that tho' the government of Kentuck had
refused to return Lamesa, yet they had offered to
make to our government a recantation, for Elseon's
crime, & to pay us almost any sum as a reparation

for our injury. The council sat silent for some time. At length the venerable Boakim arose.

I must beg, says he, the indulgence of your majesty, & this honourable council for a few moments. Never did I rise with such impressions of the high importance of our deliberations, as what I now feel. The great question to be decided, is peace or war. If peace can be preserved with honour, then let us maintain peace, but if not, let us meet war with fortitude & courage.

As to the great Crime of Elseon, no one presumes to present an apoligy. Even their own government acknowledge that he had been guilty of a great Crime. But is it of such malignity as to require the conflagration of towns, & cities & the lives of milions to make an expiation? Can no other reparation consistent with justice and humanity be received? Or must we compel in order to have an atonement made for the crime of Elseon compel the government of Kentuck to commit another crime to separate, to tear from each others embrace the husband & wife? Such a reparation as this, we cannot in justice expect. Shall we then accept of no other? Cannot our bleeding honour be healed without sheding blood without laying a whole Empire in ruins? Such refined notions of honour may prove our own ruin, as well as the ruin of those on whom we attempt to execute our vengence The calamities of war have a reciprocal action on the parties. Each must expect to endure a portion of evils. how large a portion would fall to our share in case of war, it is not for us to determine. While thirsting for revenge, we contemplate with

infinite pleasure, their armies routed, & their warriors
bleeding under our swords their women helpless &
children expiring by thousands, & their country in
flames. But reverse the scene. Suppose the enimy
have as much wit, as much stratagim, courage,
strength & inhumanity as what we you possess, &
such may be your situation. When the floodgate is
once opened, who can stop the torrent, & prevent
devastation & ruin. We ought therefore It was never
designed by the great & good Being that his children
should contend, & destroy that existence which he
gave them. they all have equal rights & ought to
strive to maintain peace & friendship. This has been
the maxim of our fathers & this the doctrine taught
by the great Founder of our government & religion.
Under the influence of this maxim, our nation has
grown to an emence multitude, & contentment & happiness have been universal. But why can we not
enjoy peace with honour? What insurmountable
obsticles are there to prevent? Why truely a recantation &—(word illegible)—are no compensation for
the injury? For other offenses these are accepted,
& why must the offense of Elseon be singular?

The Emperors daughter we presume is happy, nor
can it be a disgrace to the imperial family that she
has married the son of an emperor, the heir apparent
to his crown. But she was to have been the wife of
Sambul, the King of Sciota We can therefore with
honour to our government accept the reparation
offered. & thus preserve the blessings of peace.
But if we suffer resentment, pride & ambition to

plunge us into a war, where will its mischiefs, where will its miseries end? As to both empires are nearly equal as to numbers & resources, I will venture to predict their eventual overthrow & destruction.

Boakim would have proceeded, but Hamkol rose & interrupted. It was impudence in the extreme, but he had much brass & strong lungs, & could be heard further than Boakim

"Such sentiments, says he, may comport with the infirmities of age, but they are too degrading & cow-ardly for the vigor of youth & manhood. If we suffer insult, perfidy & outrage to pass with impunity, we may afterwards bend our necks to be trodden upon by every puny upstart, and finical coxcomb. No. Let us march with our brave warriors into the domin-ion of Hamboon. This effeminate & luxurious Court will tremble at our presence & yield the fair Lamesa unto our possession. But if they should still have the temerity to refuse, we will then display our valour by inflicting upon them a punishment, which their crimes deserve. Yes, our valiant heroes shall gain immortal renown by their heroic exploits. & by the destruction of all shall who Sciota will ever after have the pre-eminence over Kentuck, & compel her haughty sons to bow in our presence. Let war be proclaimed. & every kingdom & tribe from the River to the Lakes will pour forth their warriors. anxious to avenge our countrys wrongs. Scarce had he done speaking. And Lakoonrod, the High Priest arose. He was in the interest of Sambul & had married his sister. He had taken great umbrage at Elseon, for saying that the priesthood had too great an assendency at the court of Hambock. And lifting up his sanctimoneous eyes slowly toward heaven, & extending his right reverand hand a little above an horizontal position he spoke.

When the laws which are contained in our holy religion are transgressed, it is my duty as High Priest of the Empire to give my testimony against the transgression. Elseon, the heir apparent to the imperial throne of Kentuck has been guilty of Robery & impiety within our dominions. He has robed this Empire of an invaluable treasure, & as his crime is a most flagicious transgression of our divine law it must have been committed in defiance of the high authority of heaven, therefore it is an act of the greatest impiety. The injury the insult & the outrage has not been committed against us alone, if this was the case, perhaps we might accept of reparation; but it is committed against the throne of Omnipotence & in defiance of his authority. No reparation can of consequence be received, except it be a return of the stolen treasure, or the Blood of the Transgressor. Nothing else can satisfy the righteous demand of the Great and good Being. He therefore calls upon the civil power to execute his vengeance, to inflict an exempleary punishment. And as it is his cause & you are imployed as his instruments, you may be assured that his almighty arm will add strength to your exertions, & give you a glorious victory over your enimies. The mighty atchievements of your warriors shall immortalize their names,

& their heads shall be crowned with never fading laurels. & as for those who shall die, gloriously fighting in the cause of their country & their God, they shall immediately receive etherial bodies, & shall arise quickly to the abodes of increasing delight and glory.

He said no more. He had discharged some part of his malice against Elseon, for saing that the priesthood had too much influence in the court of Rambock. The door was now opened & it was seen that Sambul at the head of a great multitude of citizens, had taken their stand in front of the house, all crying with a loud voice, Revenge & war. Long live the Emperor & King. We will avenge their wrongs. This uproar & the harang of the high Priest determined the wavering mind of the Emperor. But the venerable Boakim & Bilhawa opposed the torrent & stood as stood firm They boldly affirmed that a war was impolitic & unjustifiabe But the Their opposition however, was in vain. The popular voice was against them & the other two counsellors Hamkal & Gammack gave their vote for war urged with great vehemence that war should be declared.

In vain were all the reasonings of the venerable Boakim & Bilhawan. The other two counsellors, Hamkol & Gamanko joining the Emperor, they proceeded to made out a declaration of war. It was in these words.

War is declared by the government & Empire of Sciota against the government & Empire of Ken-

tuck.  The Sciotans are required to exterminate with
distinction of age or sex all the inhabitants of the
Empire of Kentuck.  They are required to burn their
houses & either to destroy or take possession of their
property. for their own use & benefit.  This destruction is demanded by the great benevolent Spirit
& the Empire government of Sciota

Signed.  RAMBOCK EMPEROR OF SCIOTA.

A copy of this declaration was given to Labanco
the brother & Envoy of Hamboon.  He demanded a
guard to defend him against the rage of the common
people, who discovered a disposition to plunge their
swords into the heart of every man whose fortune it
was to be born on the other side of the River.
Labanco was guarded as far as the River & conveyed across in safety.  He repaired to Gamba
& there he proclaimed the intelligence of the declaration of War & there made known all the proceedings
of the Sciotan government.

Fond Parents

I have received two letters the 10th jan
1812 the last mentioned Mr. Kings dismission from
you, wich no doubt is great trial to you Christian
Minister is great loss to any to any people - - - -
teaches us the uncertainty of all sublinary enjoy-
ments & where to place our better trust & happiness

NOTE OF COPYIST.—The above fragment of a letter is all
that appears on page 132, after which the next leaf, pp.
133–4, is missing.  The narrative then goes on thus.

Hambolan, King of Chiauga was the next proud chief
who appeared at Tolanga, with a chosen band of
warriors.  He had fifteen thousand who boasted of

superior strength & ability. Their countanances were fierce & bold, being true indicators of their hearts which feared no danger. They were always obedient to the orders of their king, who always sought the most conspicuous place for the display of his valor. Possessed of gigantic strength & of aston-ishing agility, he was capable of performing the most brilliant achievements, which would almost exceed belief His mind was uncultivated by science & his passions were subject to no restraint. His resent-ment was quick & fiery & his anger knew no bounds for expression Nothing was concealed in his heart, whether friendship or enmity, but always exhibited by expressions by expressions strong & extravagant. He had a soul formed for war. In the bustle of the campaign in the sanguine field where heroes fell, beneath his conquering sword his ambition was grati-fied & he acquired the highest martial glory.

Ulipoon King of Michegan received the orders of the Emperor twith with great joy War suited his nig-ardly & avaricious soul, as he was in hopes to obtain great riches from the spoils of the enimy. Little did he regard the miseries & destruction of others, if by this means he could obtain wealth & agrandize himself. A mind so contracted & selfish, was not capable of imbibing one sentiment of gen-erosity or humanity or even of honour. None however, were more boisterous than he for war. None proclaimed their own valour with so loud a voice. Yet none were more destitute of courage & more capable of treachery, baseness & cruelty. Yet

with the sounding epithets of patriotism, honour &
valour, he proceeded with great expedition to collect
a chosen band. of dauntless warriors the consisted of
Eighteen thousand warriors.  Their martial appearance entitled them to a commanded of more generosity & valour than the nigardly & treacherous
Ulipoon.

Nemapon, the King of Cataraugus made no was
prompt to comply with the imperial requisition.
Tho' he prefered the scenes of peace & being very
fond of study & of the mechanical arts, his mind
was replenished with knowledge & & he took
great pleasure in promoting works of ingenuity.  He was famed for great wisdom & subtlety
penetration of mind. was capable of forming great
plans & of prosecuting them with great vigour & perseverance.  He was deliberate & circumspect in all
his movements, but was always quick on any sudden
emergency, to concert plans & to determine. had the
full command of his mental powers in every situation.  & even when dangers surrounded him, could
instantly determine the best measures to be pursued.
He prefered the scenes of peace, but could meet war
with courage & firmness.  At the head of a select
band of Seventeen thousand men, all compleatly
armed & anxious to meet the foe, he marched to join
the grand Army.

Not far behind appeared Ramack, the King of
Geneseo.  With Furious & resolute, he had made the
utmost expidition to collect his forces.  Nor did he
delay a moment when his men were collected & pre-

pared to move. At the head of ten Thousand bold
& robust wariors, he appeared at the place of general rendezvoz, within one day after the King of
Cataraugus had arrived. He bosted of the rapidity
of his movements & tho he commanded the smallest
division of the grand army, yet he anticipated distinguished laurels of glory, not less than what would
be obtained by their first commanders.

When these kings with their forces had all arived
at Tolanga, the Emperor Rambock ordered them to
parade on a great plain. They obeyed & and were
formed in solid coilums. The Emperor then attended
by his son Moonrod, his Counsellors & the high
Priest presented himself before them. His garments
glittered with ornaments, & a bunch of long feathers
of various colours were placed on the front of his
cap. His sword he held in his right hand & being
tall & straight in his person, & having a countenance
grave & bold, when he walked his appearance was
majestic. He was the commander in chief & such
was the high esteem & reverence, with which the
whole army viewed him, that none were considered
so worthy of that station. Taking a stand in front
of the army he brandished his sword. All fixed their
eyes upon him & gave profound attention. He thus
made an address.

Brave warriors. It is with the greatest satisfaction
& joy, that I now behold you assembled to revenge
one of the most flagitious Crimes of which man was
ever guilty. Ingratitude & perfedy, seduction &
Robery, & the most daring impeity against heaven
have been perpetrated. within our dominions. The

young Prince of Kentuck is the monster who has
been guilty of these Crimes. Our most amiable
daughter Lamesa he has seduced, & contrary to our
will has transported her into his own country. Wishing to avoid the effusion of human blood, we offered
to withhold our revenge, if the Emperor of Kentuck
would restore our daughter. But he has refused.
He has implicated himself & all his subjects in the
horrid Crimes of his son. Their whole land is now
guilty & every man woman & child are the proper
objects of severe chastisement. The great & Good
Being is indignant towards them, & views them with
the utmost detestation & abhorrence As we have
received our power from him he requires that we
should not only avenge our own wrongs, but likewise
execute his vengeance on the perfidious ingrates &
monsters of wickedness & impiety That this is his
divine will has been clearly investigated by our holy
prophets & priests, who have given us the most
indubital positive assurance that success shall attend
our arms. that we shall be enriched with the plunder of our enemies. that laurels of immortal fame
will crown the achievements of our warriors, & that
they shall be gloriously distinguished on the plains
of Glory. like suns & stars in the firmement of
heaven. Our cause is just, the celestial powers
above are on our side. they have brandished theis
swords & sworn that blood shall deluge the fair land
of Kentuck. You have done well my Brave warriors
that you have assembled around the standard of your
Emperor. I will conduct you to the field of battle &

direct your movements. My son Moonrod, whose arm like mine is not enfeebled by age, will mingle with the boldest combatants & lead you on to victory. By the most valorous exploits by blood & slaughter, we will convince our enimies that we are not cowards & poltroons. Their ridicule & derision shall be turned into mourning & lamentation. & we will teach their effeminate & luxurious government not to despise the hardy & brave sons of Sciota.

In full confidence that we shall gloriously triumph & add immortal lustre to our names, we will now march forward we will & avenge the injuries done to the honour of our imperial government & the rights of our Empire & all the celestial beings above shall rejoice in the execution of divine vengeance.

He said no more. The whole army with one voice proclaimed Long live the Emperor. We swear that he shall never find us Cowards & Poltroons. The Emperor then ordered them to march by divisions & each king to lead on his own subjects. They began their march toward the land of Kentuck. Their provisions & baggage were borne on the backs of mammouth. Each man had a sword by his side & a spear in his hand. & on their breasts down to their hips & on their thighs they wore peices of mammouth skin to guard them from arrows & the weapons of death. & on their Caps they wore bunches of long feathers. Their garments were short so as not to encumber them in Battle. Thus equipped & mounted, they moved on in exact order until they arrived at the great River. Here they halted to provide boats to transport them across. Their baggage & provision were borne on the backs of their mamm mammouth, which carried prodigious loads

And here we will leave them for the present & take a view of the proceedings in Kentuck.

When Labanco had presented to Hamboon the Emperor of Kentuck the declaration of war & related the proceedings of the Sciotan government he immediately assembled his counsellors who unanimously agreed to make the most active & vigirous preparations for war. The Emperor sent forth his mandates to all the princes of his Empire requiring them to assemble the most courageous warriors in their respective kingdoms & to march to the City of Gamba. All the princes of the Empire were quick to obey the requisition of their Sovereign. The army assembled & paraded on a great plain before the City. Hamboon attended by his two sons Elseon & Hanock, & by his counsellors & three of his principal priests, walked out of the city & presented himself before his army.

His garments were of various colours & his Cap was adorned with a bunch of beautiful Feathers, which waved high in the wind. In his left hand he held a spear & in his right a sword. His countenance was bold & resonute, & such was his gracefulness & eloqution, when he spoke that all eyes were fixed upon him. & all ears were attention.

Brave warriors My brave sons says he, I extremely regretted the necessity of calling you from your peaceful employments to engage in the bloody scenes of war. But such is the violence the malice & ambition of the Sciotan government that nothing will satisfy them but hostilities between the Empires. They have proclaimed war even a war of extermination against our dominions. Nor was it in our power to prevent this most dreadful calamity, unless we tore asunder the bond of wedlock between the prince & princess of the Empire. & transported her like a Culprit into their dominions. This was the only alternative which they offered to accept, to prevent this terrible crisis. & why the rigor of this demand? Was it because the young Prince had violated any law either human or divine? No; it was because the King of Sciota had fallen in love with the Princess, & wished to have her for his wife. But as she viewed him with the utmost hatred & disgust, he has been disappointed. To gratify his malice & revenge, he has roused the Sciotans to take arms, & threatens to deluge our lands with the blood of our citizens & to lay our country in ruins. It is a war on their part to gratify malice & revenge & nothing will satisfy their malignant passions but our compleate extermination. On our part it is a war of self defense of self preservation, a defence which will extend to our wives & our children, & to all the blessings & endearments of life. We must either submit to behold our dearest friends expiring in agonies our property torn from us & our houses in flames & our dearest friends expiring in agonies & even like cowards suffer them without resistance to cut our own throats or we must meet them like men determine to vindicate our rights, & to retaliate all their intended mischiefs. Nor need we fear the event of the contest. Infinite benevolence will reward our situation. & grant us that assistance which will give success to our efforts. You, my brave sons will be inspired with courage, your hands will be strong for the Battle & their warriors will fall before you like corn before the reapers sickel. With all their mighty boasting & high confidence in their superior cunning & prowess, they are men formed of the same materials which we possess. Our swords will find a passage to their hearts, & the vital blood gushing forth they will fall prostrate at our feet. Let us march then with courage to meet the implacable foe, determined either to die gloriously fighting or to obtain victory.

Having thus spoken, the whole army with a loud voice replied, Victory or death. Lead us on to victory. At the head of this army which consisted of one hundred & fifty thousand men, he marched toward the great River. They arived at the bank & beheld the Sciotas all busyly employed in making preparations to cross the River.

The Empress, the Princess Lamesa, & the Emperors daughters attended by a few friends & their servants arrived at the place where the army was encamped. As soon as Elseon heard the news of their arrival, he hastened to the place & found the company had alighted at an house & that Lamesa & her friend Holika were in a room by themselves. As soon as he entered Lamesa arose. The gloom & anxiety which were for a number of days displayed visible in her countenance at his appearance were dispelled. He received her into his arms with an affectionate embrace, & expressed the greatest pleas-

ure at seeing her once more. The tears ran down
her cheeks, for a moment she was silent, she raised
her head & replied. O Elseon, were it not for you I
should be the most wretched being in existence, & yet
my love for you has been the cause of all my present
affliction. If I had never seen you, those horrid
prospects which now present themselves to my view,
would never have been. But you are innocent, nor
am I guilty of any crime. Buth how can I endure to
behold the calamities which must fall upon both
nations in consequence of our connection? Two
empires at war, spreading carnage & ruin, warriors
bleeding on the field of Battle, innocent women &
children perishing in the agonies of death, & towns &
cities in flames. Ah horried prospect. Have you &
I my dear Elseon produced these dreadful calamities?
Is our conduct the cause which must We are not says
he, my dear Lamesa responsible for for the horrid
effects of malice & revenge which may be occasioned
by our innocent conduct. If men will be so indignant towards each other, because we do right as to
massacre & do all the mischief they can, we may
deplore their weakness & depravity, but have no more
reason, to make ourselvs unhappy on that account
than if these effects were produced by some other
cause. They alone are responsible for their crimes &
have reason for unhappy reflections.

But how can I endure, says she, to see my dearest
friends become each others implacable enimy? To
see them mutually engaged to destroy each others
life? My Father for whom I ever had the greatest
affection, & my only Brother are now at the head of

one hostile army, & your father & you my dearest husband are at the head of the other. When these armies meet, should you not plunge your sword into the heart of my Father & my brother, & would they not do the same by you if in their power? When such scenes present themselves to my view, they pierce my soul like dagers. & produce the keenest anguish. O that I could fly to my Father & on my bended knees implore forgiveness.

Yes, says Elseon, when you have done that, he will give you to the mighty Sambul for his wife.

No, never says she, never would I submit. I abhor the monster more than ever. He is the most malignant scoundrel in existence. To gratify his revenge whole Empires must be laid in ruins. What punishment more just than that he himself should fall in battle. & endure the agonies which his vengeful soul is bringing on others? But as for my Father & my Brother, they have by his artifice been deceived. I conjure you if you have any regard for my happiness, not to take their lives if in your power. Rather than that my hands should be stained with the blood of your dearest friends I will present my bosom to their swords. There lives, says he, are safe from my sword, but hark, there is an alarm. An expres arived & informed him that the Sciotan army had found means to get their boats down the River in the night unperceived, & had landed without opposition about three miles below them the Kentuckian encampment Elseon then embraced his wife & said when your protection & my own honour call I must obey. He left her in tears imploring heaven to protect him, & runing swiftly to the army he took his station.

## CHAP. XIV

HAMBOON mounted on an eligant horse richly caparisoned, rode thro the encampment proclaiming aloud, every man to his station. Seize your arms & prepare for Battle. All his princes quick to obey his commands instantly repaired to their respective divisions. & gave orders to form their men into solid collums. When this was done, they marched a small distance to the pl & paraded on the great plain of Geheno. They were now prepared for the hostile engagement. Their officers of the highest Ranks marched along their in front of their divisions & by their speeches they inspired the men with boldness & courage. They ardently wished to behold their enimies, & to have an opportunity of displaying their valour in their destruction. Hamboon then commanded his principal officers to assemble around him. When they were collected which was in front of the army, he thus addressed them.

I wish for your opinion my brave

NOTE.—Pages 143 and 144 are missing.

& heroic commanders had each a chosen band of warriors, who were ordered as soon as the battle should begin to march between the divisions & charge the enimy. in order to break their order & throw them into confusion The design of this arrangement was to break their ranks & to throw them into confusion.

The command of these bands were given to Elseon, Labanco Hanack & two counsellors of the Emperor, Hamul & Taboon. The momentous period had arived. Each grand army were now ready, were anxious for the combat, & sanguine in their expectations of obtaining a glorious victory. Musicians with instruments of various kinds were now playing thro' every division of both Armies. They blowed horns pipes & a kind of trumpet, & beat with sticks on little tubs whose heads were formed of parchments. The melody was truly martial & calculated to inspire each warrior with an ardent desire for battle & the most daring heroism. All was hushed. The musicians fell back in the rear. There was a perfect silence thro' both armies. Each Emperor with their swords brandishing rode were in front & facing their respective armies. Near three hundred thousand spears were glittering with the reflection of sunbeams. Not a cloud to be seen in the east. The sun shone with unusual brightness, in the west a dark cloud began to arise & distant thunder was heard to rumble. Hambock proclaimed with a voice which was heard from the right to the left March march my brave warriors, & fight like heroes. Hamboon saw them beginning to move but not changing his countenance, which was placid & bold, he proclaimed, Stand firm my brave sons  Let your arrows fly thick against your enimies as they advance & finish with your spears & your swords their destruction. The Musick again played & both armies gave a tremendous shout. Spears & swords

When the Sciotans had advanced with a firm &

moderate step, within a small distance of Hamboons
army, they both armies discharged arrows with with
such unerring aim & celerity that many brave warriors on both sides fell prostrate. Others were sorely
wounded & retired back in the rear. Their places
were immediately supplied & the second Rank coloped
& took their stations in the front. Each man fixing
his spear horizontaly & about as high as his breast
the Sciotans rushed forward with heroic yels & horrible shoutings & made a most tremendous & furious
charge upon the Kentucks. They received them with
firmness & courage spears met spears & many were
bent or broken & others were thrust on both sides
into the bodies of heroes. whose blood gushing forth
they fell with horrid groans pale & lifeless on the
sanguine plain. Neither army gave back, but being
nearly equal as to strength & numbers they poured
forth upon each other with a lavish hand the impliments the weapons of death & destruction Determined to conquer or die, it was impossible to
conjecture which Emperor would have gained the
victory had the divisions or bands in the rear of each
army remained inactive. But anxious to mingle
charge with the boldest warriors, the Kentuck bands
led on by their heroic princes rushed between the
divisions of the grand army & made a most furious
charge on the Sciotans. They broke thro' their
ranks, piercing their indignant foes with deadly
wounds. Heroes fell before them & many of the
Sciotans being struck with surprise & terror, began
to retire back. But the bands in the rear of their
army instantly rushed forward, & met their furious

combatants. The battle was now spread in every
direction. Many valiant chiefs who commanded
under their respective Kings, were overthrown &
many thousand robost & brave warriors, whose
names were not distinguished by office, were compeled to receive deadly wounds & to bite the dust. It
was Elseons fortune to attack the division led by the
valiant Kamoff. He broke his ranks & killed many
warriors. While driving them furiously before him,
he met Hamkol at the head of many Thousand Sciotans. Hamkol beheld the young Prince & knew him
& being fired with greatest rage & thirst for revenge,
he urged on the comabat with the most driving violence. Now, he thot was a favourable chance to
gain immortal renown. Elseon, says he, shall feel
the effects of my conquering sword. The warriors
on both side charged each other, with incredible
fury, & Elseon & Hamkol met in the centre of their
divisions. I have found you says Hamkol perfidious
monster, I will teach you to rob our Empire of its
most valuable treasure. He spoke & Elseon replied.
Art thou Hamkol, the counsellor of Hamback Your
advice has produced this blood & slaughter. Hamkol raised his sword & had not Elseon defended himself from the blow he never would have spoken again.
But, quick as the lightning Elseon darted his sword
thro' his heart Hamkol He knashed his teeth together
& with a groan tumbling headlong with a groan
expired.

The battle raged. Labanco attacked the division
of Sambul. His conquering sword had kiled two
chief & his band performed the most brilliant exploits

Sambul met him & like an indignant panther he sprang upon him & while Labanco was engaged in combat with another chief Sambul thrust his sword into his side. Thus Labanco fell lamented & beloved by all the subjects of the Empire of Kentuck. Hamack His learning wisdom & penetration of mind, his integrety firmness & courage, had gained him universal respect & given him a commanding influ- ence over the Emperor & his other Counsellors. He was viewed with such respect & reverence that the death of no man could have produced more grief & lamentation & excited in the minds of the Kentuck a more ardent thirst for revenge. The officers of his phalanx exclaimed Revenge the death of Labanco. Even lightning could not have produced a more instantaneous effect. With tenfoldrage & fury his warriors maintained the conflict & redoubled their efforts in spreading death & carnage. Even The mighty Sambul trembled at the slaughter of his sub- jects warriors & began to despair of victory he began to fearing that his intended revenge was turning upon his own head. During this slaughter of Sambuls forces Hamack was engaged in battle with Habelan King of Chiauga. No part of the war raged with a more equal balance. Warriors met warriors with such equal strength & courage, that it was impossible to determine on which side was the greatest slaughter, even their heroic chiefs prudently avoided a combat with each other & emploid their swords in overthrow- ing those of less distinction. The field was covered with the bodies of heroes besmeared with blood, which was spread thick on every side. In the mean time Hamul & Taboon who led on the other reserved divisions of the Kentucks were fiercely engaged in spreading the war thro' the ranks of the Sciotans Hamul compelled to the division commanded by Sabulmah to fall back, but still they fought as they slowly retreated, & being rein forsed by a body of troops in their rear, they continued the conflict & maintained their position. The slaughter was emence & each party boasted of the most brilliant atchievements.

Taboon made his attack on the division of Ulipoon, commanded by Hamelick. The Sciotan ranks were broken & they must have fled in confusion had not Rameck supported them with his division, warlike band. The contest now became bloody furious & equal feats of valour were displaid by contending heroes. The thirsty earth was overspread with the dead and dying bodies. of thousands & saciated their its thirst by copious draughts of human blood. Hamelick himself was slain, but not until his sword was crimsoned with the blood of his enimies But The dubious war appeared at last determined. Hamback beheld his army giving ground on every hand. He rode throout their divisions & endeavored to inspire them with persvering courage. But in vain. They could not withstand the impetuosity the numbers & strength of their Enimies. Aided by the advantage they had obtained by the arrangement they had made to manage the conflict. The Sciotans began to retreat. Such was the situation of both armies that they

the Sciotans must have principally been to overthrow
& destroyed if the Kentucks had been permitted to
continue the havoc & slaughter they had begun. But
how often are the most sanguine expectations disappointed by the decrees of heaven. At this awful
period whilst the atmosphere was repleate with the
multifarious sounds of the clashing of swords &
spears, the playing melody of the martial musick
- - - - the shouts of the conquerors & the shrieks &
groans of the dying, even then the heavens were
overspread with clouds of the most sable hue, which
had blown from the West. The thunders roared
tremendously & the flashes of lightning were incessant.
The wind began to blow from the west with great
violence the hail poured down from the clouds & was
carried with great velocity full in the faces of the Kentucks. They were unable to see their enimy, or
continue the conflict. Hambock & his princes immediately rallied their retreating forces & facing round
encouraged them to fight courageously since the
great & good Being had miraculously interposed in
their behalf. The Kentuck army were unable to
continue the conflict. they were obliged in their turn
to retreat. but such was the violence of the storm
that the Sciotans could not take any great advantage
of the confusion of their enimies. They however
pursued them to the hill which had been in the rear
of the Kentucks, overthowing and kiling some in
the pursuit. But as the hill was overspread with
trees, which broke the violence of the wind Hamboon
commanded his men to face their pursuers, The Sciotans finding that their enimies had the advantage of

the ground, & being intolerably fatigued with the battle, which had lasted near four hours retired a small distance back, & as soon as the storm abated, they marched beyond the ground which was strewed thick with the slain. Thus ended the great battle on the plain of Geheno. Both There they encamped & as the storm had now subsided, both armies proceeded to make provision to refresh themselvs, being nearly exhausted by the fatcagus fatigues of a most bloody contest, which had lasted nearly five hours. That day afforded them no time to bury their dead. The sun did not tarry in his course, but hid himself below the horizon, & darkness spread itself over the face of the earth. The warriors with their spears in their hands extended themselvs upon the earth, & spent the night in rest & sleep. Next morning they arose with renovated vigour Their thots were immediately turned to the sanguine field. Many warriors say they, lie there pierced with mortal wounds & covered with with blood. Their spirits have assumed etherial bodies, & they are now receiving the rewards assigned to the brave on the plains of glory. But they demand of us that we should secure their remains from the voracious jaws of carniverous beasts animals by intering them in the earth. But how can this be done unless both armies will mutually agree to lay down their arms during the interment. of the remains of their respective warriors. Hamboon dispached a messenger to Hambock who agreed to an armistice for the term of two days, & that ten thousand men might be emploid from each army in

burying the dead. It was indeed a melancolly day.
The conquest was not desided. Neither army had
gained a victory, or had reason to boast of any
superior advantage obtained or any heroic atchievements which were not matched by contending war- .
riors. an emence slaughter was made. Hear one hundred thousand were extended breathless on the field.
This was only the beginning of the war & what must be
the dreadful calamities if it should continue to rage?
If a few more battles should be faught, & the enfuri-
ated conqueror should turn his vengeful sword
against defenceless women & children & mingle their
blood with the blood of heroes, who had fallen bravely
fighting in their defence. When both armies viewed
the the emence slaughter that had been made of their
respective friends, instead of cooling their ardor for
the war it only served to encrease their knowledge &
their thirst for revenge.

Ten thousand men from each army without arms
marched to the field where the battle was faught, &
having selected the bodies of their respective warriors, they carried as many of them together as what
could be done with convenience & then diging into
the ground about three feet deep & throwing the
dirt around in a circular form upon the edge of the
grave they then deposited the bodies in it. covering
the ground over which they had dug with the bodies
& then placing others upon them until the whole were
deposited. They then proceede to throw dirt upon
them & to raise over them a high mound. In this man-

ner they procceded until they had finished the interment The bodies of the chiefs that were slain were
carried to their respective armies, & porforming many
customary solemnities of woe, they were intered &
prodigious mounds of eart were raised over them.
After the funeral rites were finished & the armistice
had expired, the hostile Emperors must now determine on further plans of operations.

The field was widely strewed & in many places thickly
covered with human bodies extended in various positions on their sides their backs & faces.  Some with
their arms & legs widely spread, some with their
mouths open & eyes stairing.  Mangled with swords
spears & arrows & besmeared with blood & dirt. Most
hideous forms & dreadful to behold.  Such objects
excited horror & all the sympathetick & compassion-
ate feelings of the human heart As both Emperors
had agreed to the suspension of arms for the purpose of burying the remains of these of the heroic
warriors, ten thousand men from each army entered
the field & began the mournful employment.  They
dug holes about three feet deep & in a circular form,
& of about twenty or thirty feet diameter.  & in
these they deposited the bodies of their decesed
heroes & then raised over them large mounds of
earth.  The bodies of the chiefs who had fallen were
carried to their respective armies, & buried with all
the solemnities of woe.  Over them they raised prodigious mounds of earth, which will remain for ages
as monuments to comemorate the valiant feats of
these heroes & the great battle of Gaheno.

After the funeral Rites were finished, & the armistice having expired, the hostile Emperors must now
determine on further plans for operation. Hamback
requested the advice of his principal officers, who
were unanimous in their opinion that it was their best
policy to retire back, to the hill, which was opposite
to the place where they landed, & there wait for reinforcements. This they effected the next night without being prevented by their enimy. Hamboon the
next day marched toward them, but not thinking it
good policy to attack them at present took possession
of the hill in plain view of the Sciotans & there
encamped with his whole army. As the Sciotans
sallied out in parties to plunder & to ravage the country, these were pursued overtaken & met by parties
of the Kentucks Many bloody skirmishes ensued with
varous success, & many feats of heroism were displaid on both sides. Wherever the Sciotans marched,
devastation attended their steps, & all classes of people without distinction of age or sex, who fell into
their hands became the victims of their infuriated
malice. The extermination of the Kentucks appeared
to be their oject, not considering that it might soon
be their turn to have such cruelties retaliated upon
themselves with three fold vengeance. They likewise
had a further object in view, hich was to provoke
Hamboon to attack the main army, whilst posted in
an advantageous situation But it was Hamboons
policy by placing garrisons in different stations, & by
patroling parties to prevent the Sciotand from plun-
dering & destroying his towns, & from obtaining provisions from his country & in this way to compel them

to cross the river or to attack his army in the posotion he had taken. While the two Emperors were thus manoevering & seeking by various arts & stratigems to gain an advantage over each other, a very extraordinary incident of heroism & the display of the most sincere & ardent friendship transpired. displayed transpired which is worthy a place on the historic page Insidents transpired of heroism & friendship. In the dominion of Hamboon there lived two young men who were bred in the same village, having minds formed for the exercise of the noblest principles & possessed of congenial tempers. They early contracted the greatest intimacy & formed towards each other the strongest attachment. They joined the standard of Hamboon & in the great battle of Gaheno they faught side by side & performed exploits equally bold & heroic they eat at the same board & drank of the same cup & in all their excursions they attended each other & walked hand in hand. As these two friends were seting in their tent one evening, Theljard who was the oldest says to Hamkon something whisper to me that this night we can perform a most brilliant exploit The Sciotans have held a great festival & until midnight they will be employed in singing & in dancing & in various diversions. Being greatly fatigued, when they lie down to rest their sleep will be sound. We may then enter their camp by slyly getting round them by their centinels unperceived & make a most dreadful slaughter. Your plan replied Hamkion is excellent. It is worthy of the character of an hero. I will join you. I will either triumph with you in the success of the enterprize or perish in the attempt. Perhaps we may atchieve a glorious deliverance to our Country by destroying our cruel enimies. They both taking their swords & tomehauks repaired toward the camp of the Sciotans, in order to reconoiter & find where they could enter & not be perceived by the Centinals. The Moon shone bright but would set about three oclock in the morning This was the time they had fixed upon to begin the massacer of their enimies.

At length all became silent, the moon disappeared & these young heroes had accomplished their plan in getting into the camp of the Sciotans unperceived. They found them lying in a profound sleep, for the fatigue of the day & revels of the night had bro't weariness upon them, & considering when they came down that the vigilence of their guards would secure them fro surprize, they slept with an unusual sound-ness, but their vigilence could not prevent an unsus-pected destruction. The Tomehauks & swords of these daring youth soon caused hundreds to sleep in eternal slumber, & so anxious were they to finish the destruction of their enimies that the day began to dawn, before they had cleared themselvs from the camp of their enimies Scarce however had they passed the last Centinal & the alarm was given. The Sciotans beheld a most terrible slaughter of their warriors, & being fired with indignation sallied forth in parties in every direction. Kelsock & Hamkoo had nearly gained the encampment of the Kentucks, & Hamkoon with a party of Sciotans had overtaken Hamko. Kelsock was so far in advance that he was

now safe from all danger. but turning his eyes round,
he beheld Hakoon seize his friend, who was attempt-
ing to defend himself against the party. Kelsock
turned instantly & runing furiously back cried, Spare
oh spare the youth, he is innocent. I alone contrived
the slaughter of the Sciotans, too much love to his
friend induced him to join in the enterprize, Here is
my bosom, here take your revenge. Scarce had he
spoken & Haloon plunged his sword into the heart of
Hamko. The young hero fell & with a groan expired.
Kelsock instantly rushed upon Haloon & darted his
sword thro' his heart. Prostrate he tumbled at the
feet of Hamkoo. But Kelsock could not long sur-
vive. A spear pierced him in the side. He cast his
eyes on the lifeless body of his friend & fell on
his lifeless body it, he embraced it & never breathed
again. Ah heroic youths, in friendship ye lived & in
life & death ye were joined.

Forty days had now expired since the two armies
had taken their different positions. Each had
received large reinforcements which supplied the
place of the slain. Experience had taught them to
use stratigem instead of attacking under great dis-
advantages & yet to remain long in their present
situation could not possibly terminate the war success fully on the part of the Sciotans. Rambock
considering the obsticles which attended the prosecution of every plan at last by the advice of Sambul
& Ulipoon, determined on a most rash & desperate
enterprize. An enterprize which would in a measure
satiate their revenge, provided that it should even
produce the annihilation of the army. As soon as

darkness had overspread the earth at night, Rambock marched his whole army toward the City of Gamba. & such was the stillness of their movements that they were not perceived, nor was it known by Hamboon that they had marched until the morning light. As soon as the Kentucks found that the Sciotans found that had abandoned the place of their encampment & found the direction they had gone, they immediately pursued them with the utmost expedition. But too late to prevent the intended slaughter & devastation The Sciotans without delaying their march by attacking any forts in their way, merely entered the vilages kiling the inhabitants who had not made their escape & burning their houses. They arived before the City of Gamba. Great indeed was the surprize & terror & consternation of the Citizens. Many fled to the fort. A band of about three thousand resolute warriors seized their arms, determined to risk their lives in the defence of the City. The leader of the band was Lamack the eldest son of Labanco. He inherited the virtue of his excellent Father & even thirsted to revenge his death, by sacrificing to his manes the bones of his cruel enimies. He posted his warriors in a narrow passage which led to the City. The Sciotan Emperor immediately formed his plan of attack. A large host selected from all the grand divisions of his army marched against them. They were commanded by Moonrod. He led them on against this galant & desperate band of Kentucks & made a most furious & violent charge upon them. But they were resisted with a boldness which will forever do honour to their immortal valour. Many

hundreds of their enimies they peirced with their
deadly weapons, & caused heaps of them to lie prostrate in the narrow passage. Such prodigious havock
was made on the Sciotans by this small band of valiant citizens who were driven to desperation & whose
only object was to sell their lives dear to their enimies. , that even Moonrod began to despair of forcing
his way into the City thro' this naroow passage.
Being informed by a treacherous Kentuck of another
passage, he immediately dispatched a band of about
four thousand from his army to enter the city thro
that passage & to fall upon the rear of the Kentucks.
This plan succeeded. These heroes now found the
war to rage both in front & rear & part facing their
new assailants, they attacked their new assailants
them with incredible fury. What could they do?
Resistance was now in vain. They could no longer
maintain the bloody contest against such a mighty
host. Lamack then commanded the survivors of his little band to break thro' the ranks of his last assailants,
& to retreat to the fort. It was impossible to withstand
the violence of their charge. They broke thro' the
ranks of their enimies, & made a passage over the
bodies of heroes, thro' which the retreated & marched
to the fort. About seven hundred with their valiant
leader thus made their escape & arived safe in the fort
The remainder of the three thousand sold their lives in
defence of their friends & their country. This battle
checked the progress of the enemy which prevented
an emence slaughter of Citizens. as the greatest part
had opportunity by this means to gain the fort. As
soon as all resistance was overcome & had subsided,

the Sciotans lost no time, but marched into the city & commenced a general plunder of all articles which could be conveniently transported. Ulipoon tho careful not to expose his person to the deadly weapons of an enimy, was however very industrious in this part of the war. None discovered so much engagedness as himself to grasp the most valuable property in the City. But expecting the Kentuck army to arrive soon, they must accomplish their mischief with the utmost expidition. The City they sat on fire in various places & then retired back & encamped near the fort intending on the next day, unless prevented by the arival of Hamboon with his army, to storm the fort & massacer the whole multitude of citizens which were there collected. Behold the conflagration of the city The flames in curls spread toward heaven, & as the darkness of the night had now commenced, this added to the horror of the scene. The illumination spread far & wide & distant vilages beheld the redning light assend. as a certain pioneer of their conflagration should the war contilnue to rage. But mark the sorrow & lamentation of the poor citizens now encircled by the walls of a fort. Happy that they had escaped the massacer of a barbarious unrelenting enimy, but indignant & sorrowful at beholding the ruins of all their property, & even filled with the greatest anxiety lest Hamboon should not arive in season to prevent the storming of the fort. But their anxiety soon vanished.

When the shades of evening began to overspread the earth Hamboon & his army had arived within five miles of the city. They beheld the flames beginning

to spread. The idea was instantly realized that an
indiscriminate slaughter had taken place. What
were the distracted outcries of the dwellers of the
city. Fathers & mothers brothers & sisters wives &
children? In addition to the destruction of all their
property, they now had a realizing anticipation of the
massacre of their dearest friends & relations. Such
was their anxiety to precipitate their march that it
was scarcely in the power of their commander to
retard their steps. so as to prevent them from breaking the order of their ranks. They determined however to make the utmost expidition, & if they found
their enimy to take ample vengence. But when they
arived & found that the greatest part of the citizens
were safe in the fort, this afforded no small allevia-
tion to their anxiety & grief. But their thirst for
revenge & their ardent desire to engage the enimy did
not in the least abate.

Determined that the Sciotans should have no
chance to improve the darkness of the ensuing night,
to make their escape, every preparation was made to
attack them the next morning. This was expected by
the Sciotans who were wishing for another opportunity to measure swords with the Kentucks. & as soon
as the morning light appeared they marched a small
distance to a hill & there paraded in proper order for
battle. Scarcely had they finished their arrangements when they beheld Hambooms army marching
towards them. He halted within about half a mile of
the Sciotans, & sent out a small party to reconoitre &
discover their situation. In the meantime he ordered
Hamack his son to march with twelve thousand men

around the Sciotan army & lie in ambush in their rear
in order to surprize them with an attack after the
battle should commence.

As the two armies were paraded in fair view of
each other the expectation was that a most bloody
engagement would take place immediately. . The
cowardly mind of Ulipoon was not a little terrified
when he beheld the numbers & the martial appearance of the enimy.   But his inventive genius was not
long at a loss for an expedient which he imagined
would extricate himself from all danger.   He repairs
to Hambock & addressed him to this effect.   May it
please your your majesty.   During the first battle it
was my misfortune to be prevented from being at the
head of my brave warriots & displying my valour.   It
is my wish now to perform feats of heroism which
shall place me on equal ground with the most valiant
princes of your Empire.   With your permission I will
lead on my division & storm the fort of the Kentucks.
This will fill their warroiors with consternation & terror.   You may then obtain an easy victory & destroy
them with as much facility as you would so many
porcupines.   Besides by attacking the fort at this
time when they are not expecting such a manoever,
the imperial family will be prevented from making
their escape & I shall then be able to restore to your
majesty your daughter Lamesa.   The Emperor being
pleased with the plan granted to Ulipoon his permission to carry it into effect.   Ulipoon did not wait a
moment.   But immediately returned back & commanded his forces which consisted of about seventeen
thousand to march.   He was careful to see that they

carried with them at the same time all the plunder
they had taken in the City of Gamba. & particularly
that portion which had been set apart for himself.
But nothing was further from the heart of Ulipoon
than to fulfill his promise. He had no intention to
risk his person in the hazardous attempt to storm the
fort. But his determination was to march with the
utmost expidition to his own diminions. & to carry
with him his rich plunder. Having marched towards
the fort until he had got beyond view of the Sciotan
army. He then ordered them to turn their course to
the great River to the place where they had left
their boats. In this direction they had not proceeded far when they were seen by a number of
pioneers whom Hamack had sent forward to make
discoveries. As his band were not far distant, they
soon gave him the intelligence. He immediately dis-
pacht an express to Iamboon, informing him that he
should pursue them as their object probably was
to ravage the country,& recommending not to attack
the Sciotans until further information from him
Hamacks division were not discovered by Ulipoon &
of consequence he proceeded in his march without
suspecting any anoiance from the enimy. happy in
the reflection that he had greatly enriched himself by
a prodigious mass of plunder & not in the least trou-
bled about his fellow warriors, whom he had deserted
on the eve of a most hazardous engagement. Hamack pursued him, but was careful not to be discovered.
When the sun was nearly down Ulipoon halted &
encamped. During the night, Hamack made his
arrangements. He formed his men into four divisions

& surrounded the enimy. Their orders were as soon as
the morning light began to appear to rush into Ulipoons encampment & to massacer his warriors without discrimination. The fatal moment had arived, &
punctual at the very instant of time, the attack was
begun on evey part. & such was the surprize & terror which it produced that the Sciotans were thrown
into the utmost confusion, & it was impossible for
their officers to form them into any order to make
defence. Every man at last attempted to make his
escape, but wherever they rushed forward in any
direction, they met the deady spears of the Kentucks.
It is impossible to describe the horror of the bloody
scene, for even humanity recoils at beholding.
Humanity sympathy & compassion must drop a tear
at beholding the uproar & confusion, the distress &
anguish, the blood & carnage of so many thousand
brave warriors. whose great isfortune was to have a
coward for their commander who were reduced to
this situation by the cowardice & & nigardly & avaricious disposition of their commander  But only
three thousand made their escape. As for Ulipoon
he was mortally wounded & lay prostrate on the field
After the slaughter was ended, in passing over the
field of the Slain Hamack beheld this illfated prince
an object truly pitiable to behold. In the agonies of
death & wreathing under the most acute pains
he explaims Alas my wretched situation. It was avarice, cursed avarice which induced me to enagge in
this horrid war & now my the mischief and cruelties
I intended as a means to acquire wealth & agrandize-

ment are justly turned upon my own head. He spoke & deeply groaning he breathes no more The galant Hamack droped a tear & feeling no enmity toward the lifeless remains of those who had been his enimies he ordered three hundred men to bury remain on the ground & commit their bodies to the Dust. This says he, is the will of him whose compassion is infinite He then directed Como his chief captain to pusue the survivors of Ulipoons army & to destroy them if possible. With the remainder of his own troops he returned back to cary into effect the order of Hamboon. Como overtook & killed about a thousand of the wretched fugitives. The remainder escaped to their own land except about fifty who fled to the army of Hamboon & gave him the dreadful intelligence of Ulipoons destruction. Great were the amazement & consternation of Hambock & & his whole army. They now beheld their situation to be extremely critical & dangerous & saw the necessity of the most vigourous & heroic exertions. What says Hambock to his princes, is our wisest Course to pursue? Sabamah, Hancoll & Wunapon advised him to retreat without losing a moment, for say they we have taken ample revenge for the crime of Elseon. To effect this, we have thrown ourselvs into the heart of their country, have lost a large division of our army & are so weakened by our losses that we are in the utmost danger of being defeated, & even annahilated. It must therefore be the hight of folly & madness to prosecute the war any further in this country But Sambul & the other other princes condemned this plan as pusilanimous & disgraceful & proposed to steal a march on the

Kentucks & to storm their fort, before be ore they should be apprized of their design. This last advice met the approbation of the Emperor, Nothing says he can save our army from destruction but the most daring atchievements. That they might gain the fort without being perceived by the Kentucks, It was necessary that they should march some distance in the direction where Hamack had encamped in order to cooperate with Hamboon, when he should commence the engagement. When the night had far advanced Hambocks forces were all in readiness & began their march for the fort. They proceeded about two miles & a small party in advance discovered Hamacks warriors. This discovery produced an alter ation in Hambocks plans. He directed Sambul to proceed against the fort, whilst he as soon as the light should appear would attack Hamack. Sambul was highly pleased with this command, as a victory would ensure him the capture of Lamesa. & afford him an opportunity to obtain revenge. He arived at the fort just as the blushing moon began to appear. Great indeed was the surprize which his arival produced. On three sides he stationed small parties, who were ordered to massacre all the citizens, who should attempt to make their escape. With the main body of his army, he made an assault upon the fort. Amazement & terror seized the minds of the whole multitude of citizens in the fort. This enterprize of the Sciotans was unexpectected, as they were were unprepared to defend the fort against such a formidable force. Lamack however placed himself at the head of about one thousand warriors, & attempted to beat them back from the wall & prevent their making a breach. But it was impossible with his small band to withstand the strength of such a mighty army. They broke down part of the palisades and entered the fort thro' the breach & immediately began the massacre of the defenceless multitude without regard to age or sex. Sambul being anxious to find Lamesa, rushed forward with a small band & surrounded a small block house He then broke down the door & entered. Here he beheld all the ladies of the imperial family & many other ladies of distinction. He instantly sprang towards Lamesa in order to seize her, but was prevented by Heliza, who stept between them & falling upon her knees implored him to spare the life of Lamesa. Scarce had she spoken when the cruel monster buried his sword in her bosom, & she fell lifeless before the eyes of her dearest friend. Lamesa gave a scream & looking fiercely on Sambul she exclaimed, Thou monster of villiany & cruelty, could nothing satiate your revenge but the death of my dear friend, the amiable Haliza? Here is my heart I am prepared for your next victim. Ah no, says Sambul, your life is safe from my sword. I shall conduct you to my palace & you shall be honored with me for your partner. Insult me not says she, thou malicious bloody villian. Either kill me or begone from my sight. My eyes can never indure the man who is guilty of such monstrous crimes. Set your heart at rest says he, my dear Lamesa. I will convince you that I am a better man than your beloved Elseon. His head shall soon satiate my revenge. & then you

shall be the queen of Sciota.  At this instant a loud
voice was heard.  The Kentucks are marching with
a prodigious army toward the fort.  Sambul turning
to his warriors present ordered them to guard the
women in that house, & not permit any of them to
escape.  For, says he, I must go and destroy that
army of Kentucks.  Great already had been the
slaughters which the Sciotians had made of the citizens in the fort.  Those who had attempted to escape
by a gate which was thrown open were met & massacred by the Sciotan warriors on the utside, but their
progress was arested by the appearance of Elseon at
the head of thirty thousand warriors.  They had
marched with the greatest speed, for they were
informed by an express that the Sciotans had invested
the fort.  When Sambul beheld them he instantly
concluded to withdraw his army out of the fort, & to try
a battle with them in the open field.  The orders were
immediately spread thro' every part of the fort where
his men were employed in killing the defenceless & in
fighting with the little band of desperate heroes,
whom Hamack commanded.  The Sciotans were soon
formed & marched out of the fort & paraded in proper
order for battle.  Elseon observing this commanded
his two men to halt, & made his arrangements to rush
forward & commence the attack.  Having brandished
his sword as a token for silence, he then spoke.

"My brave warriors," The glorious period has
arived, for arived us to display our valour in the
destruction of our enimies.  What monstrous cruelties have they perpetrated?  Behold your city in
ruins, listen to the cries of your murdered friends

whose innocent blood calls for vengeance. Consider
the situation of those who are surrounded by the walls
of yonder fort, how many thousand are massacred,
& how many must share their fate unless you fight
like heroes. By our valour we can effect their deliverance & rid our land of the most disgraceful mur-
derers that ever disgraced humanity. Their standard
is that of the Sciotan king. whose malice & vengeful
disposition have produced tis horrid war. Urged on
by his malignant passions, he has engaged under-
taken a most desperate & mad enterprize. He has
thrown himself & his army into a most critical & dangerous situation

Fight as you did at the great battle of Gaheno & your
enimies will lie prostrate in the dust, & your name
shall be illustrious. Rush forward my brave warriors, & let your motto be victory or death.

Not a moment when his warriors were stimulated
for the combat did Elseon tarry, but marched with
precipitation prepared to make a most furios charge.
Sambul was ready to meet him, & marched forward
with equal boldness & celerity. The charge was tremendous. not the dashing against each other of two
mighty ships in a hurricane upon the boistrous ocean
would have been more terrible. Each warrior fear-
less of danger met his antagonist, determined to
destroy his life or loose his own in the contest. The
battle extended thro every part of both armies. As
warriors fell in the front ranks their places were supplied from the rear. & reserved Bands rushing
between the divisions were met by others of equal

strength & valour. Helicon, the intimate friend of
Elseon beheld Sambul who was encouraging his warriors to fight bravely. As no other alternative
remained for them but victory or death. When
Helicon beheld him, his youthful mind felt the
impulse of ambition. He sprang toward Sambul &
challenged him to the combat. Sambul gave him
no time to repeat the challenge but rushed upon him
with more fury than a tiger. & with his sword he
struck Helicons head from his body. Thus fell the
brave the amiable youth, whose thirst for glory
impeled him to attempt an exploit too rash & daring.
Warriors fell on every side & the field was covered
with the dead & dying heroes. A messenger ran &
told Elseon of the fate of Helicon who commanded
the left wing of his army & that Sambul had broken
the ranks & was making indiscribible havock of his
warriors. What intelligence could have been more
shocking. Elseon could not refrain from tears for a
moment. Ah Helicon says he, thou hast been more
dear to me than a brother. Heaven demands that I
should avenge thy cruel death. He instantly selected
a small band & marched with the utmost speed to the
left wing of his army. he ralied his retreating warriors & engaged in the conflict with tenfold fury. Soon
he beheld the mighty Sambul whose sword was crimsoned with the blood of his friend, & Sambul cast his
eyes upon him & as he beheld him his malice instantly
inkindled into such a furious flame that his reason
fled for a moment & he raved like a madman. both
heroessprang towards each other. Their warriors
beheld them & being mutually inspired with the same

sentiments the respective bands retired back, & left the two indignant champions in the space between.

Ah ingrate exclaimed Sambul. Robber & perfidious scoundrel, after securing the Emperors daughter & who was my wife & transporting her from our dominion have you the temerity to meet my conquering sword? This sword which pierced Labanco & cut of the head of Helicon & which has destroyed hundreds of warriors more mighty than yourself, shall be plunged into your cowardly heart, & your head shall be carried in triumph into the City of Tolanga, & there it shall be preserved as a trophy trophy of my superior strength & valour.

Vain boaster says Elseon I rejoice to meet you; that The Benevolent Being will now terminate your career of bloody crime. This sword shall pierce your malignant heart, & cut of that head which has ploted the ruin of my country.

Sambul eager for revenge could hear no more He sprang forward aimed a thrust of his sword at Elseons heart but Elseon turned the point of his sword from him with his own & then darted his sword into his left arm. which caused the blood to gush forth. Sambul was now more indignant than ever. & raising his sword he threw his whole strength into one mighty effort with the intention to divide his body in twain, but Elseon quick as the lightning sprang back & Sambuls sword struck the ground with a prodigious force, which broke it in the middle. He himself had nearly tumbled his whole length but recovering & beholding his defenceless situation, he ·

ran a small distance, & seizing a stone sufficiently big
for a common man to lift, he threw it at Elseon. It
flew with great velocity & had not Elseon bowed his
head his brains must have quited their habitation.
His Cap however was not so fortunate. Having met
the stone as he bowed it was carried some distance
from him & lodged on the ground. Elseon regardless
of his Cap ran swiftly upon Sambul whose feet having slipped when he threw the stone had fallen upon
his back & had not recovered. Spare oh, spare my
life says he, & I will restore peace to Kentuck & you
may enjoy Lamesa. No peace says Elseon, do I
desire with a Man, whose sword is red with the blood
of my friend. He spoke & plunged his sword into
Sambuls heart. The Sciotans beheld the huge body
of their King pale & lifeless. Consternation & terror
seized their minds. They fled in dismay & confusion.
Elseon pursued them with his warriors & overtook &
killed thousands in the pursuit. About two thousand
made good their escape, & carried the doleful tidings
of Sambuls death & the slaughter of his army to their
own land, & indeed their escape was owing to the
great anxiety of Elseon & his warriors to visit their
friends in the fort & to ascertain the extent of the
massacre that Sambul & his army had made. After
pursuing the Sciotans about six miles Elseon & his
army returned in great haste & entered the fort.
Great inexpressibly great was the joy of the citizens
when they beheld them re-turning with the laurels of
Victory. & when they were informed of the destruction of so many thousands of their enimies. But as
great was the grief & lamentation when they beheld

& reflected on the vast number of citizens & of Elseons warriors who had fallen by the sword of the
Sciotans.    But no death produced such universal
regret & sorrow as those of Helicon & Heliza.    The
one was the intimate friend of Elseon & the other of
Lamesa.    They both possessed hearts which were
formed for the most ardent friendship & love.    Their
acquaintance produced a sincere attachment.    They
exchanged vows of perpetual fidelity & love to each
other, & only waited for the termination of the war to
fulfill their mutual engagement, to unite their hands
in wedlock.    But their pleasing anticipation of conjugal felicity was destroyed by the cruel sword of
Sambul.    Naught availed the innocence & the amiable accomplishments of the fair Haliza.    She must
fall a victim to satiate the revenge of a barbarous
tyrant.    Had Helicon known when he attacked the
savage monster, that he had had assassinated his
beloved Heliza, it would have inspired him with the
added desire for revenge & added vigour to his arm
& keenness to his sword.    Ah, said A Kentuck bard
represented the etherial form of Heliza as arriving on
the celestial plain, & being told that she must wait a
short time & Helicon would arrive & conduct her as
his partner to a delightful bower which was surrounded by the most beautiful flowers & delicious
fruits, & where they singing of musikal birds would
charm them with their melody.

When Elseon had entered the fort he found that
Lamack with his little band had made prisoners of
the Sciotan warriors whom Sambul had left to guard
the imperial ladies, & that the Sciotans had done

them no injury nor even insulted them with words. Says Elseon, for this honourable treatment of my friends I will show these enimies compassion. Go, says he to them, return in peace to your own land, & tell your friends that Elseon will not hurt an enimy who has done him a favour. The time of Elseon was precious. He spent but a few moments with Lamesa, in which they exchanged mutual congratulations & expressions of the most tender & sincere affection. She conjured him to spare the life of her father & brother & not to expose his own life any farther than his own honour & the interest of his country required. I shall cheerfully says he, comply with every request which will promote your happiness. He embraced her, & bade her adieu. As the situation of Hamboons army might require his immediate return, he lost no time to regulate matters in the fort. But leaving five thousand men to bury the dead and attend the citizens he marched with the remainder which consisted of about twenty thousand to Hamboons encampment. When Sambul marched with his division against the fort, it was Hambocks intention to have attacked Hamack the next morning, but perceiving that Hamboon had been apprized of his movements & was then within a small distance ready to cooperate with Hamacks division, Hamback altered his plan & determined to wait for the return of Sambul. As for Hamboon he concluded to wait until Elseons return. These determinations of the hostile Emperors prevented for the time any engagements between the two grand armies. But when the fate of Sambuls division was decided & Elseon had returned with the joyful news of his victory, the Kentucks were all anxious for an immediate Battle.

NOTE.—This was found with the foregoing manuscript and in the same handwriting.

But having every reason to place the highest confidence in your friendship & prudence I have no reluctance in complying with with your request. in giving you my sentiments of the christian Religion. And so far from considering the freedom you take in making the request impertinence I view it as a mark of your high esteem for me affectionate solicitude for my happiness. In giving you my sentiments of the Christian religion, you will perceive that I am not trameled with traditionary & vulgar prejudice that I do not believe certain parts & certain parts & certain propositions to be treu merely because that my ancestors believe them & because they are popular. In forming my creed I bring everything to the standard of reason, that intellectual This is an unerring & sure guide in all matters of faith & practice. Having divested myself heretofore of traditionary & vulgar prejudice, & submiting to the guidance of reason it is impossible for me to have the same sentiments of the christian religion which its advocates consider as orthodox. It is in my view a mass of contradictions. & an heterogeneous mixture of wisdom & folly, nor can I find any clear & incontrivertible evidence of its being a revelation from an infinitely benevolent & wise God. It is true that I never have had the leisure nor patience to read the elaborate & varied productions of divines

in its vindication. every part of it with critical attention or tostudy the metaphysical jargon of divines in
its vindication. It is enough for me to know that
propositions which are in contradiction to each other
cannot both be true, & that doctrines & facts which
represent the supreme being as a barbarous & cruel
tyrant can never be dictated by infinite wisdom.
Whatever the clergy say on the contrary can have no
effect in altering my sentiments. I know as well as
they that two & two make four, & that three angles
of a triangle of a triangle are equal to two right
angles. But notwithstanding I disavow any belief in
in the divinity of the Bible, & consider it as a mere
human production designed to inrich & agrandize its
authors & to enable them to manage the multitude.
Yet casting aside a considerable mass of rubbish &
fanatical rant, I find that it contains a system of eth-
. ics or morals which cannot be excelled on account of
their tendency to amiliorate the condition of man. &
to promote individual social & public happiness & that
in various instances it represents the Almighty as
possessing attributes worthy of transcendent character, having a view therefore to those parts of the
Bible which are truly good & excellent I sometimes
speak of it in terms of high commendation. And
indeed I am inclined to believe that notwithstanding
the mischiefs & injuries which have been produced by
the bigoted zeal of fanatics & interested priests yet that
such evils are more than counterbalanced in a Christian land by the benefits which result to the great
mass of the people by their believing that the Bible is
of divine origin. & that it contains a revelation from

God. Such being my view of the subject, I pre fer my candle to remain under to remain under a bushel, nor make no exertions to dissipate their happy delusion, as

> NOTE OF COPYIST.—On the other side of the paper on which the above is written & in what seems the same hand is the following:

Itham Joyner privlg to erect Mill, & the pvlg of wtr. Wright has prefern & he next.  To fix to take out wtr for himslf & to be at one ¼ expense of keeping dam in repair.  If wishing to sell to gv Wrt pvlg buing if dont buy to sel to another his works but not pvlg of wtr I. Joyner & W. Brigham agree to build a house for their use.  Sd B. to 6 feet on the water below the width of the house & J to have for six feet & B. to 12 feet on the same side in the rear bank & 12 feet of the garret. to be at equal expense in the water works. To be at equal expense in the partitions of the rooms.

*The Writings of Sollomon Spaulding Proved by Aron Wright Oliver Smith, John N Miller & others. The testimonies of the above Gentlemen are now in my possession.*         Signed

D. P. HURLBUT.